About the Author

Kim Shell lives in a small seaside town in County Down with her son, Jack. Taking inspiration from the places she travels and the strangers she meets along the way. She enjoys nature, photography, animals and her job as a self-employed dog groomer. This is her first novel.

Trial to Triumph

Kim Shell

_____

Trial to Triumph

Olympia Publishers
London

www.olympiapublishers.com
OLYMPIA PAPERBACK EDITION

A CIP catalogue record for this title is
available from the British Library.

ISBN: 978-1-84897-841-6

First Published in 2018

Olympia Publishers
60 Cannon Street
London
EC4N 6NP

Printed in Great Britain

Dedication

I would like to dedicate this book to a great teacher, Mr Killen from Lagan College. Thank you for teaching me to write and showing me the joy it could bring me. I finally finished one. I wish you could have read this.

Also in memory of My Steven who was a one in seven billion kind of guy.

Acknowledgments

With thanks to Jen Hova, Rebecca, Robbie, Sheila, Professor Page, Miss Stevenson at Priory College and countless others. Thank you for your help.

Prologue

Love can be a great menace. It can be as powerful as a raging dragon and as directionless as a lantern in the wind. It makes sensible people in any world, in any culture, do foolish things. Not so very long ago a strong willed queen-to-be fell madly in love with two brothers. Both of them were charming and seemed to care for her greatly. There was no doubt in her mind, that they were both besotted with her as she was with them. As time went on and her coronation date grew closer, she had to decide which one to marry. She loved them both but as tradition dictates she chose the older brother as he was to inherit the most money. She didn't need his fortune however it did add to the royal treasury.

After the marriage, the affection he had shown proved to be false. He wanted to control her and quash all her personality; he wanted the power of a king and did not want to share it. He hated her for being the one born royal instead of him. He grew rapidly crueller refusing to allow her to visit friends, family or even royal events without him. He fired her loyal maid and replaced her with a woman he was having an affair with. This woman would report everything back to him.

The Queen grew weaker, smaller, and more timid as time went on. Those who were close to her watched her deteriorate at an astounding speed. Concerned for her safety the other brother, who was more true than his sibling, came to visit her. Even after a marriage of his own he knew that he could love no one the way he loved her. While difficult, they met in secret. At first they met just to talk, but then their love grew too powerful and they began an affair. They knew it was wrong. When the queen became pregnant, she finally admitted to herself that it was time to end it.

"This could start a war," she lamented while staring at the pink, white and yellow blossoms fall from the trees onto the peaceful water.

"Anything could start a war," he responded. He wanted to look into her eyes, but instead found himself staring at the tranquil blue of the water.

"We could be the reason for a war. I'm not prepared to risk the safety of the country for us," she allowed the tip of her fingers to circle the back of his strong hand. He turned his hand around and grabbed hers to plead with her.

"Love is the most powerful magic there is and I love you. We deserve happiness just like the people you protect. You should not stay with a man that you do not love simply because you feel it is your duty. You are the queen. Your people love you."

"My heart tells me to protect you and my people. He will kill you and our child. I'd rather live a life with a man I hate and keep you alive, than live a life without you,"

"He will kill our baby,"

"Not if he thinks it is his,"

That was one of the last conversations she had with the man she truly loved. Over the years she had come to regret her hasty marriage. She would pine for her soul mate with every breath she took and with such a passion it surely would have killed her; had she not been brutally murdered.

One warm October afternoon, in another part of the kingdom of Gandros, a woman by the name of

Alicia Dovinpoir was admiring the beauty of the land. She had always found autumn to be a refreshing time. It was full of hard work, but it was a time to enjoy the last of the sun. It was a time to throw leaves with her son, hope that they didn't kick any snakes at each other and splash in the puddles. It was a time to hear the laughter; for there is no greater sound to a loving parent than that of a child's laughter. That sound can drown out the sorrows of the world even if it's just for a moment.

On this crisp day, when the air was just cold enough to catch the back of your throat, Alicia Dovinpoir looked round to see her pride and joy covered in the warm milk she had spent an age squeezing from a cow. She liked to call the cow Rosie, her husband liked to call it stinky, or pooie if baby Leo was nearby, as it made him laugh. Alicia picked up her pudgy son and smiled. There were not many mothers in these trying times that could say their two year olds were verging on fat. She knew she should probably scold him for tipping over the bucket, but she was unable to do so. The sight brought her too much joy and after all, there was no need to get angry over spilt milk.

Alicia entered her modest stone cottage. It was a white washed building with ivy growing along the walls so thick it was quite possibly the reason the house never felt as cold as expected. It was also the reason the windows were getting smaller every year. It had a well maintained thatched roof complete with an abandoned birds nest. The whole building was framed with flowers, not just on the ever decreasing window sills but on the porch in pots with simple designs. Alicia and her husband had agreed that any land they had must be used for a purpose. So they only planted food in the ground, but the flowers were just as important in Alicia's eyes. She believed that seeing beauty on the outside and all around would remind people of the beauty that people had on the inside. In times when many people struggled to provide for their families, the smell of a well-placed flower can at least give a pause to the torment. Alicia hoped that if her son grew up and one day left home, as most men will, he will come across a flower like the ones she had planted and he will think of home and remember he is loved. She went in to bath her son, nothing smelled worse than a toddler covered in stale milk, except a toddler covered in stale milk who had just had an accident.

When he was dry, she went to the porch and sat on her wicker rocking chair with her patchwork quilt and gazed at the beauty of her home while knitting socks. Alicia always thought that one could never have enough socks.

She admired the rolling hills and the fields in the distance where her husband was working tirelessly for the landlord to provide the comforts they enjoyed. It was hard work, but country life was invigorating and worth the labour.

Overhead a dragon raged passed, "War is brewing Leo, that's another dragon on a hunt. There have been many more escaped prisoners than I ever recall. We are safe here my boy, royal matters do not concern us,"

The boy started to laugh heartily and struggled to climb down the few steps as he saw his father arrive. He giggled as his father threw him in the air and caught him again with his strong muscular sun burned arms. Leo had inherited his father's blonde hair and strange eyes. One eye was a deep piercing blue while the other was a terrifying orange. Strangers often gave Mr Dovinpoir a wide berth in the street as it was often said, by those who believed in such superstitions, that he could easily be mistaken for a minion of evil, for everyone knew that the darkness marked its followers. A person could be marked in many ways: such as a birth mark anywhere on the body, or an unexplained scar, or different coloured eyes. Evil likes to sign its work, everyone knew that, but Mr Dovinpoir was far from malevolent. Alicia had always been much more kind of heart and believed that darkness of a person's soul was much more subtle but war and famine brought about a strange paranoia and even people that knew him well caught themselves being more wary. They often wondered why he had such luck.

It was unusual for him to be home before dark, as his hard working attitude had always saw his family through hardship, and Leo wanted to enjoy the unexpected time with his father, however when Mr Dovinpoir looked to his wife she knew instantly that something was wrong. She followed him inside, the ominous feelings growing. She offered him his dinner, which he gratefully took, as she put a stroppy baby Leo to bed. When he was asleep she joined her husband at the table.

"My love," he began tentatively, "I have been called to serve my king. There is fear of trouble brewing and I must leave tonight. I do not wish to be apart from you and I will write to you as often as I can and I'll send you my wage. With luck, the fear will amount to nothing and I will be home in a year. I love you, my soul mate; I will visit you in your dreams to make sure you sleep well and to let you know that I miss you and Leo every day,"

It all happened too fast. He gathered what little he needed and left her; walking into the now setting sun with dragons soaring overhead. Their hearts ached. She longed for him to turn around and look at her once more, but alas, he could not bear to let her see the tears in his eyes.

That was the beginning of it all.

Chapter One

Not a bird could be seen in the blood stained sky. Not a breath could be heard down in the scorched city of Gandros. Once bright and cheerful clouds were now transformed into figures of death and destruction. The once magnificent city was now turned to ash, a shadow of its former beauty. Looking down from the dragon's eye, no one was there except the bodies and spirits of the ill –fated; innocent children and their mothers. Men lay mortally wounded, scattered about like weeds in the breeze. Blood covered the lands and filled every crevice; the stench of death could be smelt for miles around. From above, dragons revelled in the decay of an ancient dynasty and the land over which they once ruled. Fires blazed. In the distance, unlikely soldiers cowered beneath the remaining archways of the Slamina stronghold. Even the vast mountains of Shaavaer had been decimated. Now a place of refuge for the wounded and surviving, its caves were a perilous last resort. The forsaken sanctuary was being brought down with the combined efforts of the deranged dragons and their riders.

In one such cave, three survivors stood shrouded in a grave darkness, each feeling the hopelessness of their world. The walls around them seemed to weep with an arctic dew. The walls mimicked the hopelessness and despair felt by all. A young girl knelt, crying at her brother's feet, while their companion looked on helplessly. She was small and delicate with fire red hair and bright green eyes -a trademark of her heritage. Any story ever told about the Slamina bloodline or any painting ever created always showed a member of the family with bold green eyes. Sometimes a peasant would be born with green eyes and they are said to be blessed with the luck of the Gods. They would grow up to be successful and it was unlucky to anger any one with green eyes. It would be like insulting the Divine directly. The young girl's eyes welled with sadness, not just of the loss of her world and kingdom, but the words that departed from her brother's mouth brought yet more despair and grief to her already breaking heart. She stared up at her brother and saw determination: unfaltering and unchanging. He wanted victory and revenge; not caring how it was achieved, so long as it was done. His battered armour made no sound as he bent down to his beloved sister. She firmly closed her eyes, convinced she would not open them. She wrapped her arms around his legs and held on tightly, as only a child can.

Alessandro was full to the brim of seemingly tireless tears. His face was dulled by the distress that had become a significant part of his life. He looked away from his sister. His eyes hung around the bottom of their sockets; he had neither the desire nor the energy to lift them. Closing his eyes added support to the dam that held back the spilling of his woes onto the shoulders of his younger sibling.

Alessandro took a deep breath, hoping for some form of fresh inspiration to filter into his heart. His hands were clenched so tight that his knuckles were protruding from the flesh which entrapped them. His jagged nails bore deeply into his sweaty palms. Blood covered the lines in his hand and dripped onto what remained of his clothes. He brought his lower lip into his mouth to try and prevent it from quivering.

He was forced to recite from his practiced script. He rested his hands on Saoirse's shoulders, transferring his blood onto her. He pushed her gently, removing her grip from his legs and raised her chin with his index finger so that he could look directly at her as he spoke. She rebelled and chose to face the eroded walls of their would-be tomb instead.

"Saoirse," he pleaded, "Please look at me."

His miserable tone of voice, the uncharacteristic show of emotion weakened her resolve. Even so Saoirse still refused to look straight at him.

He sighed and stared into the darkness of the trembling cave. A short distance away a dragon roared and the screams of yet more victims of the slaughter echoed through the stone like a siren, warning them that the smoke had arrived, and the fire was nearing. Saoirse's eyes shot towards the noise, she stared transfixed for a while at the direction from which it came. Then Alessandro, his head was low, his eyes closed, drew a shaking breath and said,

"Saoirse, I know you must be scared about going into the other world without me but I have to keep you safe,"

"How can you keep me safe if we are apart? Ales please don't … please just… this is my home," Her heart was breaking as she spoke.

"We are the last of our bloodline and it is the only way I can keep you safe until the war is over. The enemy want you. They want to do something so horrid it doesn't bear thinking about,"

"What do they want with me, Ales. I am not even next in line. You are. If you told me then maybe I would understand."

"Thalious will watch over you. You trust him don't you?" The third member of the trio just gave her a smile, trying with all his might to appear confident.

"I will make sure you come back but not until the time is right. Don't you understand?"

"No I don't and that's what I keep trying to tell you. I don't understand!"

Alessandro looked to Thalious, who simply shrugged his shoulders helplessly and gave him a hopeless look with his hazel eyes and gritted his teeth as a tear fell.

"I promise you Saoirse, I will make this right. I will get my revenge for this injustice, you have my word, and a man of pride is nothing without his word!" He pulled her close and hugged her tight, "Besides How can I hope to rebuild this land without the royal princess. I'll need your magic touch and royal smile wont I?"

Another ear-splitting howl came gushing through the slim vent at the top of a pile of collapsed rock at the entrance to the cave. Alessandro began another valiant attempt to make his sister understand. He stared at Saoirse, observing her youthful ignorance longing for a more carefree time burdened with the knowledge he kept from her.

"We must hurry! I don't know how long we can remain concealed."

He hesitated trying to decide whether or not to divulge the true nature of their parent's fate, or indeed how to explain this final piece of traumatic truth. He decided it was time and there was no other way to say it, no way to sugar coat the facts, no way to make it easier on a child's ears. Times of war call for the need for our young to be hardened, however cruel it may be to rob a child of youth, it was the only way she could survive. This was more difficult to him than finding out for himself; he wanted to protect her from everything.

Alessandro had been passing the room where his parents were deep in slumber and had seen to his horror a discuali fosocatus enter   his parent's throats. To the untrained eye a discuali fosocatus looks like an innocuous dull blue grey dust particle. However, those blessed with residual powers of enhanced sight from the ancestors can see the distinct detail of its worm like core, surrounded by an   ethereal   cloud.   That   particular   breed   of the discuali species enters the throat of its victims and once in the lungs it multiplies the poisonous toxins that are naturally in its light weight body. It then releases them, leaving it immobile as it dies with its victim. There are many theories on how to remove them before irreversible damage is done. Though because the creature, as a precautionary measure, usually only attacks when the victims are asleep, the targets are unable to defend themselves making the chances of a successful kill much higher. Death of a sleeping victim can occur within four minutes of the creature entering the body.

Alessandro had tried desperately to wake his parents but his attempts proved futile. He remembered the feel of the crisp morning air rushing past his face as he fell to his knees, strangled by emotion. He was ashamed at how unprepared he was not just for death, but for war and betrayal. His father had always told him to expect the unexpected. He remembered how he had raised his trembling hands to remove the talisman, a piece of family history, from around his father's neck. The discuali had been dormant for many years. They didn't kill without orders. Someone had found out how to control them and had used them to assassinate his parents; bringing about a war that was rapidly spreading across the globe.

"I think you should have this. It is a symbol of our heritage and bolsters my belief that we have the right to protect this land and lead it back to prosperity. This necklace had a hidden power that my mother could not tap into. Many have tried over the generations since the great war with the Hoggronn Xzenny. It is believed that our ancestors used all the magic that the necklace held to banish these power hungry savages from our land and force them to live in seclusion, but it still proved that our ancestors earned the right to rule."

He then reached around his own neck and removed the concealed golden necklace. It had a dragon rearing on its muscular hindquarters with exceptionally realistic fire billowing from its inanimate nostrils.

"It is made from a substance called Ultina. It contains scrapings from the horn of a unicorn and oil from the mouth of the last recorded wild dragon. You and I are the last of the Slamina bloodline. Protect it."

He stood up to his full height towering over his sibling; he seemed to show no doubt in his convictions. She saw it in his eyes; he was going to force her to go into another world on her own. Saoirse felt she was being discarded, that her voice was not being heard.

A tear fell down her darkening face as she made her final plea. She was under no illusion as she began her statement as to the likelihood of its success. She felt trapped like a captive fish in a tiny bowl, able to see the events that were taking place around her but enclosed behind the shatterproof glass of youthful dependence. She was unable to help. That was the sad fact of being eight years old; even if she were more mature than most. She understood her brother's opinion, though that was far from enough to prevent retaliation.

"Why won't you bring me home? If I stay, I promise to learn to fight. To kill if I have to! Like you!"

He growled and started shouting, startling Saoirse with his violence. His voice was harsh and dominating.

"Saoirse! You do not hear my words and if you do, you choose to ignore them. I DO NOT WISH FOR YOU TO STAY, NOR DO I WANT YOU TO KILL. I'm doing this because it needs to be done. I won't have you in the way of harm and I will hear no more of your disobedience!"

Saoirse knew deep down that she would be a burden, and although a childlike part of her was desperate to continue, she did not want to infuriate her brother before their inevitable separation.

Alessandro hooked the necklace around Saoirse's small neck and just looked at her. He most probably would never see her again. The odds of survival were very slim, but the benefits outweighed the risks. He was proud that Saoirse wanted to fight and he relished the thought of being a role model for her.

He turned and took five lengthy steps to the exit and crouched down, scanning the area with his keen vision. A close distance away he saw to his deep distress the monster that had come to haunt his every living moment; a Glugular dragon. It had a sense of smell that far exceeded any other creature in the world he knew of.

He attempted to disguise his uneasiness at the sight of the rich soil brown scales that covered the animal's compact gleaming body. Its tail tip was bright scarlet, a sign that it had recently shed blood. Yet more fear arose in his mind as he thought that the majority of these dragons were covered from tail tip to hip; after all, it was a war and many lives would have been stolen.

It was Alessandro's belief that it had been trained to track a distinct scent. When Alessandro's father had been ruling, these dragons were rarely released. The only time their services were required was to capture run away prisoners who were a danger to civilians. Unlike other dragons that could be used for transport or ceremonial purposes. The rest of their lives were spent dormant, in a coma like state. The reasoning behind their captivity was that they were hard to control, even for their expert handlers. When they awoke they were hungry and in a blood thirsty frenzy. However, their superior hunting skills made the risk necessary.

The demon was a physical form of fear itself. It had pale, pulsating violet eyes with minute yellow pupils. Its gigantic merciless wings sent out gusts of wind with every slow, wary beat. Every hair on the trio's arms rose as though they could feel the concentration of the animal and its rider, intent on finding survivors.

Without warning the dragon stiffened to a halt. It stood stark still with the armoured rider clutching tightly to the red hot chains which trapped the evil being into servitude. The sinister figure wore armour that was black in colour to match his bleak soul. Printed on each arm was a single red ring, worn only by the elite dragon trainers, servers of the realm.

The violet in the dragon's eyes transformed into a restless red. It ominously rotated its head in their direction. Its snail like speed and heavy draws of breath created a sense of extreme trepidation. Had it caught their scent? Alessandro's eyes narrowed. He appeared to be making eye contact with the animal as it hovered rigid, mid breath, suspended in the air. He tried to read its movements, preying it turn and flee. He wasn't ready for this. It was too much. It was too soon. He silently made a plea to the Gods that he knew would never be considered.

Alessandro turned abruptly to face both his sister and Thalious. He was so confident that he could trust Thalious to watch Saoirse, but he couldn't help taking what could be a final look at a good friend. Thalious was part dwarf and in being so, had inherited a small muscular body. Despite the malnutrition and starvation they had all endured, Thalious was still a daunting sight. He had a compact stocky build with bulging muscles. His hair was long and rough, tangled beyond repair and so thick with dirt and blood no one could remember the colour of it.

He had in his possession an item which gave away a terrifying element of his nature, an object that he carried with him at all times. It's carved bone handle, which was believed to belong to his departed brother's corpse, was bound in animal leather to remind him that his enemies were nothing more than prey to be hunted. The head itself was double edged; an axe head on one half added heft to the keen blade which extended past the grip of the handle to a sharp point on the other side.

Thalious registered the unspoken fear in Alessandro's face. He was aware of what was expected of him and tried with all his might to convince himself he was prepared. Breathing heavily, he said,

"Your majesty! It is beyond me to understand your daring methods or question why you refuse to flee what others would consider an impossible battle, but I will fulfil your wishes to the best of my ability. I pray this is not the end and that we will meet again in your glorious victory."

"No matter what the outcome, my heart and soul belong here and they shall remain here, always!"

Saoirse couldn't hold back her fear; she ran to her brother, held onto him and wept once more.

"You cannot make me leave! I will not leave you to die alone!"

Saoirse was grasping tightly to her brother's legs. Her tears trickled down his dull armour leaving glimmering paths that revealed the cool steel beneath the grime. Alessandro picked her up with ease and hugged her affectionately.

"Do not fear! Don't ever fear. I am watching over you."

The temperature rose. He swiftly and without warning threw her to Thalious. A dragon's dilated pupil was clearly visible above the rubble and as if in a trance, Alessandro's strained voice bellowed,

"Trolex Vaetev!" he disappeared into the atmosphere, no body, no ash, Alessandro was gone.

Thalious knew that there was a chance that Alessandro could die any time he performed magic. Magic was not as easy as many people believed. There was a lot of math involved. For every piece of magic that was cast the person doing the magic would have to take the energy from somewhere else, that could be water, trees, sunlight, food, but if the spell was more powerful than the energy available nearby then the extra power would be taken from the casters soul. Magicians, (who were usually members of the royal family) knew that energy could not be created; only transferred from one use to another. He was frightened, but he knew what he had to do.

In sight of Thalious and Saoirse, a portal stood just within reach. Saoirse screamed and ran towards the point where she had lost her brother. A flame burst through the caves opening and seemed to slow down as she ran at the oncoming threat. She was hit by a searing power and flew backwards. Burnt and unconscious she lay barely alive.

Thalious acted without pause so as to avoid another blast. Within a fraction of a second he had drawn his axe level with his shoulder in Saoirse's direction. Fear gave strength to his voice and he bellowed,

"Lat Mey!"

He threw himself into the portal, with Saoirse floating alongside him. Its mystic hues and hypnotic swirling engulfed their bodies, and all was gone, with no evidence, other than the charred walls that anyone had been there.

Chapter Two

After the fire burnt out, Alessandro stood with his head hung low, his limbs weak and his hands clawed, exhausted but miraculously undamaged.

He stood for a moment, trying to recall what had happened. It came to him in flashes, which made him feel as though his head would split in two. He had seen the dragon, felt the terror and remembered what the elders had taught him about absorbing magic from a dragon's breath. You can't store it but you can use it. You must use enough of the power so that you are not burned or killed, if you try to use too much power, your soul will be consumed to obtain the extra energy. This form of magic was only taught to the royals to prevent peasants and potential rivals from using it to their advantage.

Alessandro's father had created laws banning the common man from performing magic after a terrible day when a group of school children were playing with magic and accidentally destroyed their souls. This was worse than dying. When someone dies their life force moves on to the next world, where he had sent Saoirse. To lose one's soul was to have everything that made you whole dispersed around the planet with no consciousness. There was no known way to sew the soul back together and help it move on. It also didn't always happen instantly. Sometimes a spell can cause a fabric of the soul to come loose and then an invisible entity pulls at it until nothing is left. It was often described to the children that if they imagined their soul was a forward moving tapestry and a bad spell caused a thread to come loose and be tangled around a nail in a fence. The tapestry or soul would keep moving but the tangled thread would pull away from the masterpiece, which unravelled more and more until there was nothing left. Now if you imagine that all souls are connected like a large patchwork of tapestries if one is weakened and disappears it has a detrimental effect on the rest of the work. The warning was told to all, but not all listened.

Alessandro had thought for a while that the portal would use the correct amount of energy. Even so, all that magic is, is the transfer of energy from one thing to another.

Alessandro had always had a keen interest in fire. He knew what it was made of. He was taught that everything is made up of several elements; Not earth, wind, water and fire, but something much more intricate, involving infinite forms of magical specks that came together in patterns shaping the world around them.

There are a limited number of these elements. They arrange themselves in different ways. Being a sorcerer of magic, meant you had to learn what something is made of and how much energy is required to rearrange them and bend them to your will. Some minds are naturally more powerful than others, though most can be trained over time.

Alessandro stood his heart as low as the depth of the ocean. He had to gather what little faithful followers remained in these harsh times. He needed to continue his education, but he had to find someone willing to do it.

Alessandro considered his options. He had dealt with Saoirse; there was no need to be concerned with her.

He pushed her face and innocent nature to the back of his mind. He could not think of her! Not yet. The dragon was a problem, a temporarily avoidable one, but a problem all the same. If it caught his scent it would attack him again, and most likely kill him as he did not know any other spell apart from the portal that would use the correct proportion of energy. He couldn't go around opening portals all over the land; a portal stays open until it is used. Alessandro was aware that no amount of flowers can hide his smell and trick a dragon but he was confident that he could buy enough time to figure out a solution.

Next problem was raising and training an army, whilst finding someone with enough skill to train him in magic. As well as that, he had to remain below the radar, as he was a wanted man in more places than just Gandros.

Alessandro knew of a tribe that had the knowledge to teach him the particular spells he needed. Several generations ago, in the great war, Alessandro's family had won the power to rule the country and the previous rulers were given the choice to become employed by them or be banished. They in their dishonest state chose exile. They had had many followers and would surely reproduce to prevent the end of their line. If Alessandro promised them freedom and status, then surely, they would help him. The question remained how did he find them? No one had seen a hint of them since they had fled. No one had taken the time to look. They were gifted in magic and many people believed that it was this tribe, the Hoggronn Xzenny that actually tamed magic for the use of mortals. He decided to set out in search of information. If he discovered what his opponent was up to he could then work on a counter attack.

The exit had widened and the rocks still held heat from the near fatal breath. Alessandro slipped through; his downcast eyes began to glisten with stars of renewed enthusiasm. He was barely suppressing a scream of rage and strode full of confidence across the rocks, stopping only once to take in the view of his failing kingdom.

He was feeling a strange sensation, it was hard to try and figure out but it was as though one moment he could see clearly, then the next moment it would become blurry and he was seeing the world as though he was watching a play through his eyes. He was finding it hard to focus and felt almost light headed. Memories started swimming into view, then leaving allowing him to see clearly again only for another memory to come shooting across his vision. He had to sit down until he could gather his composure. It had been a very strong spell and it took a lot of energy.

He sat looking down at the dilapidated streets and the ruins of his memories. He saw it as it was now; littered with corpses in various stages of decay, blood, vomit, and bones. He also saw himself as a boy with his best friend weaving in and out of the hard working merchants. In his mind's eye, memories were unfolding in front of him. He could feel the texture of the cloth the cloaks were made from as they whipped past him. They darted past the ordinary people and heard the shop keepers howl like wolves, territorial of their stalls. He heard the chatting of the older women as he paused to parade in front of them, flattering them with his childish charm.

He knew that the stall holders would not harm them, but when an unsightly bulk of a man caught his cousin by the wrist, the danger was all too real for him. He drew his sword and threatened the villain. Knowing what would happen to him if he didn't show deference to royalty, the butcher reluctantly released the boy.

The two youths ran to the foot of an old willow tree they had claimed as their own.

"Alessandro?" Troy had begun, still panting.

"Yes," he gasped.

"I want to thank you."

"I'm sure you would have done the same for me."

"Not for that. When my parents died I was alone..." Seeing Alessandro defend him had brought up some unwelcome memories and a need to ensure that Alessandro knew how important he was.

Alessandro made an attempt to interrupt Troy; even at this young age, he had hated what he considered softness.

"No wait, please. Before they died my mother forbid me to even think of you. Your parents took me in even after all the horror my family put them through," Troy didn't know all the details about the feud but he knew that the King and Queen had taken pity on him and adopted him.

"You are like a brother to me. In a way I am glad they parted from my life and I feel like a traitor for it," Troy anxiously awaited Alessandro's response.

"You are my best friend Troy and I would lay down my life to protect you."

"If you do that I will be killed for causing the death of the future king and your death would be in vain!" he smiled.

It was hard for Alessandro to accept these fast changing times. Troy had been Alessandro's only real friend. It made his heart heavy to stare down at the war zone as it was now, knowing that he was battling the only person that truly knew him.

He started off again on his trek through the jungle of emotions and decomposing corpses. He kept his eyes on the ocean and tried with all his might to ignore the gentle crunching on the blood drenched roads and the horrific stench of needless, guilt filled death. A noise in the distance made Alessandro quicken his pace.

The feeling of walking over the charred remains of children was more than Alessandro could bear. He stopped on numerous occasions to throw up what little he had in his stomach. On one such occasion he felt a cold chill run the entire way around his spine; twisting, turning as though his blood had turned to brittle ice and was coursing through his body.

He looked behind him and saw nothing, so he allowed his gaze to fall. For a horrifying moment he was convinced that the skeleton of a young boy was gripping his ankle. It took him a while to collect his thoughts and realize that the boy was alive. His body was starved and filthy, his skin burnt with both fresh and healing wounds, but he was alive. He used Alessandro's shocked body to pull himself into an upright position. The pathetic form somehow paralyzed Alessandro. The way the boy's bones stuck out from his thin flesh and the effort of his weak muscles, straining with exhaustion had grasped Alessandro's attention. He wanted to pull away, he willed himself to step back but couldn't. In the boy's hand, was a finely decorated blade, probably stolen from one of the upper class bodies.

Alessandro was ashamed of his inability to defend himself from such a pathetic opposition. He should be adapted to this by now. The boy placed the blade directly at Alessandro's throat. They were eye to eye. Those eerie eyes, one a shocking blue and the other an unnatural orange, Alessandro would dream of these eyes often. The look of murderous hatred is not easily forgotten.

When the boy eventually spoke, it was a barely audible growl.

"It's your fault she's dead!"

The boy was ten maybe twelve years old and the only thing that kept him alive was hatred. He repeated the accusation over and over as though his mind was broken into a continuous loop.

He stared at Alessandro's throat, with a hunger one so young should not have. All he needed to do was flick the knife and watch the blood spurt, but he wanted him to suffer, to feel great pain.

"You don't think I'll do it but I will. She is dead because of you! So I should kill you! Avenge her!"

His shaking became more violent. His head kept twitching with the conflict that was taking place in his head. He seemed to be talking just as much to himself as he was Alessandro.

"I should kill you now!" he raised his head with new eagerness.

At this point Alessandro snapped out of his trance and stepped back.

"Who is dead? I can assure you that these deaths are neither my desire, nor my complete doing. If you explain to me what happened I may be able to help you find some justice."

Alessandro tried to hide his guilt. He felt as though each of his organs were being ground to dust. He knew he was partly responsible at least, but deaths were inevitable in war. His negative thoughts were destroying his ability to rationalize.

As more words were on the verge of being spoken a young girl or woman (Alessandro could not tell her age), scuttled out of the shadows and put her arms around the boy. She looked as though she had been looking for him for a long time. When the boy did not move or acknowledge her presence she followed his eyes and for apparently, the first time noticed Alessandro was standing there.

"Come Leo! There will be another time, a better time. Please don't let her death be in vain."

She tried frantically to get the boy to run on his own steam, as she was not strong enough to carry him away. Whilst talking to the boy, her eyes never left Alessandro. Those eyes were familiar to him but he could not recall where he knew the girl from, and found that all he could do was stare straight back at her.

She was taller than a man. That is to say she was taller than Alessandro himself. Her feet were a considerable size and fresh blood flowed from them. Alessandro took a sharp breath in disgust at the realization that she had no toe nails. On closer inspection she had no fingernails either. It was a vile sight. She had heavy bags under her eyes and was as pale as death itself.

Alessandro felt certain he should say something.

"If my intentions were to kill you, I would have done so already," he tried to smile to prove he had no evil intent.

This did not have the desired effect. A flicker of abhorrence crossed her face. She stood as straight as she could and snarled.

"There will come a time that you will regret threatening me, 'Lord Slamina'," at that she turned to the boy, "Leo, think of that darn dog you rescued. You know that if you don't come with me now I will eat her myself," at that she finally succeeded in moving the boy. They fled neither to the sea nor the mountain.

Alessandro was utterly perplexed. He wanted to run after them, but they would only fear him more. It bothered him that he could not place the girls face.

Intense thoughts were shooting through Alessandro's brain. A child a little older than his sister considered him to be the sole cause of this catastrophe. How could it be that his quest had turned into an attempt to not only save his life against his enemies, but to defend himself against the people he had sworn to protect? It was a heart wrenching fact that few people had trust or even the slightest belief in his intentions. He trailed through the unbeaten paths with little enthusiasm in himself and his abilities. The people he cared for were either dead, in another world or trying to kill him. How could this happen? How could he not have foreseen it?

With the passing of both time and thought, Alessandro's body grew wary. Though he was walking, his feet did not lift to the same level. He was dragging his feet leaving evidence that could be tracked. His scent was strong due to the amount of sweat from his illness. The grass he walked on fell forward not backwards which proved it was a human path. Alessandro admitted defeat against the natural order of sleep and rest. He retreated to a forested area which he had been trying to avoid, mostly because he was not yet well enough for a battle with any of the beasts that lurked in the shadows of its canopy. He stayed on the edges, not deep enough in to be viewed as a threat, though his body was embedded far enough in the plant life to be camouflaged from passers-by. He did not feel secure, he did not want to fall into a deep slumber, though no matter how much his mind protested his body dominated and he fell into a coma like state.

Chapter Three

When he awoke, the day was new and the land was quiet. Even the burrowing insects completed their daily rituals in an unusual fashion as if they too had increased security. The ants, king of insects went about their work with fear in every movement. Alessandro looked to the sky; the stars had retired and let room for the sun to carry on its duties. The sun rose slowly. It too feared to witness this revolting time. Imagine seeing everything that went on in the world; the good and the bad, only the horrid sights are magnified and the joyous ones are suffocated into submission. What deeds were taking place that struck terror in the hearts of the immortals? The air was calm, perhaps a little too still. When the wind makes no sound or movement it makes travelling unnoticed a difficult task your slight mishaps, your overturned stones, your unhidden footprints. None of these can be disguised by wind activity.

Alessandro walked along the edge of the forest in the shade of the trees until he reached the top of a hill where there was an almost vertical slope to the edge of the sea. He lowered himself so that his body was the height of a small child. He did not place his knees on the ground as that would make flight slower.

The view was something to be awed at for hours, if one had the time. In all the sorrow this sight was a blessing. The Loch was tinted with the reflection of the rising sun, orange, and a colour that signifies both anger and hope. The sun could be seen creeping up in the centre of the gap between the edges of the land that framed the water. On the edges of the land there stood a volcano on each side. They had been dormant for many years but every so often there would be a warning rumble to remind people that the land may be fertile and steep, which provided shelter but it came at a price. The trees on the sloping hill were tall and bare of branches for the lower half. Above this the branches fell in layers out of human reach. The sight of the ships drew Alessandro into a pensive mood.

He had flashes in his mind of what this place meant to him now, and what it had meant to him during the days of his faded youth. It had always been a sanctuary for him, a place outside guarded property. It was a thinking spot where he had always looked on in wonder at the warriors. Part of him at that age had thought that men went out to fight purely for the glory and the honour. That was until the moment when his childish romanticized views had been harshly injected with a foul dose of reality. Alessandro had never until that point seen injured soldiers return from a battle. Usually, they went out to war defeated the enemy and occupied the defeated territory. He did not deny, it may have been harsh and some would say wrong to defeat and steal foreign land; but his home was under constant threat and the only way to eliminate that threat was to reduce the ways in which they could be attacked and the people who were likely to consider it. They did not take prisoners and were not cruel to barbaric standards. On the day of the disillusionment, Alessandro had witnessed the arrival home of a small fleet of ships, looking battered and barely sea worthy. They returned moving slowly like a dying cat trying to find somewhere to rest its head for its final moments. This was not what Alessandro had been expecting. They had not lost a single battle since the day of his birth.

When he had reached the hill where he now stood, he had not witnessed the joyful banter of successful homesick soldiers, but a crowd of drained, blood soaked men, carrying each other out of the ships. It was not the blood of those they had defeated but their own. While some men were in a make shift stretchers, others were hobbling alongside them. The bodies of the fallen warriors had been left behind to rot on foreign soil, save a few that had been dragged aboard the ship to give their families piece of mind.

At a distance just visible from the top of the slope, it was possible to see another tragedy. A marvellous ship, one of the largest to return was sinking. People were in the water swimming with all their might against the pull of the ship, but the men were weak. Their minds were full of dread which poisoned their muscles. Their cries were barely audible and yet they echoed in the hearts of every living man. That image would stick with Alessandro till the day he died and beyond.

The stench for weeks after was unbearable as bodies, bloated and mutilated kept coming ashore. The graves were quickly filled, so many of the men were dumped into an unmarked pit. When it was full the bodies were burned. It was such an undignified end for so many good men.

Now the dock was full of ships ready to go out to war once more. They wore their flags high, their sails fresh and undamaged, the guards however stood in stark contrast weary and exhausted, their shoulders slouched and backs bent after a night's watch. They were due to change over and return to their sleeping quarters for what they thought of as a well-earned rest.

These were Troy's troops. A sickening, caustic rage deep inside Alessandro rose like a volcanic blast. His hatred was reaching boiling point. He knew he had to wait. His only hope and way, to find out what Troy was planning, was to board a ship, dangerous as that may be. If he accomplished this goal, he could try to gather followers. He knew he couldn't just walk onto a ship no matter how tired the guards were. They would surely wake at the sight of him. Their anger, though not quite so passionate was not a force to be underestimated.

He slid down the steep hill as quietly as he could, hoping to be as discreet as a house spider. Not unexpectedly his activities were noticed, and a handful of men were sent to investigate the origin of the descending stones, whether they were of animal causes or traitorous pauses. Alessandro had expected a group of scouts. After all, it was always a mistake to under value the competence of your opponent. He managed to avoid most of them and tried to look as camouflaged as possible. He was filthy and his clothes were no more than rags, and his armour was rust, but he was still not quite invisible in the growth. He heard footsteps near him and tried not to move, praying he would not be seen. He felt like a child playing hide and seek only attempting to hide in plain sight.

When the steps were almost above him his nerve caved. He unsheathed his sword and leapt to his feet. He was on the verge of thrusting the sword through the most convenient and easily accessible part of the man that was threatening his survival, though milliseconds before his metal made a mark, his movements lost momentum.

"Dylan!" Alessandro was confounded. Dylan had been Alessandro's tutor. To see him on the opposite side ready to strike him down was torture. He tried to ready himself for such betrayals. The art of turning heart to stone, was one skill he had not yet mastered.

"Quiet Alessandro or it will be your head and not just your tongue that will be removed!" He was never one for pleasantries, but Alessandro was confused. Was he friend or foe?

Dylan whistled a high pitch almost screeching sound.

"Dylan, what are you doing? Are we to fight? I thought that you of all people would honour a one on one duel."

"Use your brain. You know I do not intend to fight you. Now stay in silence."

Within seconds Alessandro was surrounded by a group of seven people. Dylan was the tallest at almost seven foot. Alessandro knew three of the members, though not in great depth. One was Adam, the father of one of the servants at the palace; he was broad with greying hair and profound frowning wrinkles. The second was the mother of a girl that Saoirse had been very sociable with. She was an attractive woman with an unconventional past. The third person was Arthur. He was a man similar in age to Alessandro and very talented on horseback. It had been he who had helped Alessandro to perfect his riding skills. He had mousey brown hair, blue eyes and a toned body.

"I believe you know Adam, Arthur and Chiara," Dylan pointed to each in turn, "This is Beth, Thomas and Andrew. We are part of the resistance. We are on your side but we work for Troy in the hope of getting so far in, that we know every detail of any plan. We assumed you would try to board a ship and knew it would be impossible for you to do so. So collectively, we have gathered a ship and supplies of our own. It is manned by those most loyal to your cause. There is still a risk that we have a spy on board, so you will need to be concealed from all. The only exceptions stand before you now!"

Alessandro was staring at him in a way that he had never done before. He had always admired Dylan, but looking at him now, had it not been completely inappropriate and in public, he would have hugged the man that stood before him, offering a solution to a major problem. Dylan had raised him to be the man he now was.

"How did you convince him you were loyal to him? How do I know that this is not some trick to lower my guard?" Alessandro had momentarily let his defences slip. This could be a trap. After all Troy had been there growing up alongside him. Dylan had aided him in his grief over his parents' death.

"You really are the most suspicious boy. I remember, I used to say you were far too trusting. How times change."

"You failed to answer my question!"

"You must learn when people are trying to help you, and not push their patience!"

They exchanged an angry discouraging glance, but Dylan sighed and explained.

"If you must know he always thought that I favoured him during the time the three of us spent together. I must say, I never expected him to be this stupid. Everyone knows that the Gods have blessed the royal line. If you try to destroy the will of the God's all will suffer."

Alessandro was having trouble believing that this was real or even possible. He wanted to believe it was true, and despite his suspicions he had no other way onto a ship and he was not in contact with any allies. If something went wrong at sea, he was at a greater disadvantage.

"If you don't mind me asking, how exactly did you know that I would try to board a ship?"

"Dear Alessandro, you are a very predictable person with very limited options!"

"Very well, how do you propose I get onto your ship?"

"We all must report back to our commanders and explain that the reason our search was lengthened was due to old foot prints leading nowhere. That means you must board the ship unescorted."

Chiara then asked him, "Are you still an accomplished swimmer?"

"I am."

"How are you at climbing?" Adam piped up.

"Adequate."

"Our ship has red sails and at its bow there is a mermaid figurehead. There is enough room for a man to climb and hide beneath the tail. We will put a rope down and you can strap yourself to it until we clear the deck. You will then take up residence in a cabin that we will have prepared and labelled out of bounds. That means no one goes in, and you don't come out,"

"In theory, it could work, but it all depends on Alessandro's agility, and no offence, but he doesn't look up too much!" This time it was a man that Alessandro did not know.

"Andrew I assure you I can make the journey. I will wrap the rope around each leg and then around my waist and through my legs again. It will be most uncomfortable, but achievable none the less."

"Very well," began Dylan, "...do not get caught boy or we will hang for it!"

With nervous anticipation the group left Alessandro to fend for himself. He watched them leave and reviewed his options. They were right, they were limited. Would Troy predict his actions as easily? His next move could be the beginning or the end.

Alessandro waited and watched without moving for what seemed an age. He needed to ensure that his possible allies had enough time to secure his passage. His fears affected his stealth as he slid down the hill, but thankfully he made it to the water's edge.

Even though the sun was high, there was a strong chill, brought in by the northerly wind. Alessandro removed what remained of his damaged armour and lowered himself into the water. It felt thick and cold. He submerged his entire body to try to adjust to the temperature. He looked across and saw the large red sails. It was strange that there was only one. He presumed no one could afford the dye, if it was dye, or take the time to do it. The weight of his wet clothes pulled him as though they had a mind of their own and were begging him not to take the chance. In his mind the taste of the water was tarnished with the memory of floating heroes. He stayed below the water for as long as his lungs permitted, rising only when the crushing pressure was unbearable.

When he reached the ship the rope was already there. He gave a silent prayer to whomever or whatever was watching over him at that moment. He stayed on the right hand side where there were no ships and stayed close to the shadows made by the bulge of wood that extended into a carving.

He wanted to rest before pulling himself up; but staying afloat was taking more energy from him, so he reached up, put the rope between his legs and around his wrists and pulled. It felt to him as though his muscles would tear apart. He somehow managed to get three quarters of the way up, and tied himself in with great difficulty. He could hear men above him, moving and gossiping. It was unnerving not knowing a friend from an enemy.

He had waited for most of the day. The cool air was getting worse. He felt drained of energy. He thought he might have the wrong ship and was even more worried when the ship began to move.

It was not going at its full pace, but that did not prevent the wind from chipping at his features causing his skin to be red and raw. It would have been more painful had it not been for the fact that his entire body was almost completely numb.

When the time came for Alessandro to enter the ship his body was limp and almost lifeless. The sunset and its reflection from the water had almost blinded him. The night air had turned his nerves to sleeping vessels. Dylan and his crew took great care in discretely pulling him onto the deck.

"Damn stupid boy!" He could only just hear Dylan's words.

"Well it was your idea!" Chiara retorted.

"Come on, just help me move him. Grab some ruddy blankets before he dies of hypothermia.

"Do you think he will be alright?"

"This flaming fool will never be alright! But he knows well enough that I would curse him to oblivion if he dies on us now! Do you hear that?" he said, tersely shaking Alessandro.

Alessandro came back to his senses long enough to understand the threat. He couldn't help but admire the rough courage of his former mentor, especially in times of stress.

"You had better keep it down. I am not getting caught because of your delirious chatter!" There was a lot of concern in his eyes but his voice refused to give any sign of it.

Alessandro was barely coherent as they carried him hurriedly, stripped him and wrapped him up again like a fragile child.

The cabin he was being concealed in, was leaking and smelt strongly of fish and urine. He wondered how long it would be before he faced scurvy or various other illnesses related to an unprepared and incorrectly stocked ship. As his fevered thoughts wandered, his ears closed to the warnings of sanity. Noises all around him took the form of strange pitches and confusing nonsense.

Every crack in the wall seemed to multiply and divide and even blur at given times. He was delirious and scared. New dangers arrived every second. All around him sounds moved, creatures crept, unknown activity everywhere. Evil was in everything he laid his eyes on.

Even the voices and faces of those who were helping him were of no comfort. His temperature had risen dangerously high. Faces began to melt, sounds were given shape, and colours had no boundaries. They just fused into one another. People's voices turned into a distorted demonic wail. Everything was a threat.

The combination of his illness and the ships motion made Alessandro vomit regularly. He had to be rested on his side because he was too feeble to turn when being sick so there was a possibility he might choke. All of the faithful seven waited nervously for the fever to break, each of them wore a heavy crown of guilt.

In an attempt to mask Alessandro's groans they moved the ships small animals into his cabin. They were mostly birds kept for meat and eggs. The dust and dirt they brought didn't help Alessandro's condition, but kept him hidden should he pull through with so little medical aid.

Chapter Four

Dylan and Chiara nominated themselves the chief carers of the birds so were down most days to check on Alessandro. It also meant that they got to decide who went into the room. It was not a job that most people wanted to do and the fact that some of the animals were making a noise similar to possession made it an even less desirable place to go. They had no idea the sounds of muffled screams were actually Alessandro. It involved cleaning the cages and maintaining the health of the animals as well as collecting the eggs and killing any of the creatures that were not producing enough food. The crew had a system for deciding who got the big chunk of meat. The captain got the first bite and after that it went through the list of winners of their games tournament. Fresh meat was worth more to them than money as the journey at sea is often long and hard and a person can grow sick of eating fish and eggs. The tournament was friendly rivalry and consisted of a lot of different challenges. It could be something simple, such as knocking a wig off a stick in the most inventive way possible, or diving off the highest point of the ship, or getting the harshest tattoo. Anyone who came up with an idea for a challenge got points on the meat board. It kept up moral and helped the people on the boat become more bonded. The closer people were the harder it would be for them to betray each other. Or so the theory was.

The group of faithful followers were amazed that Alessandro was still alive. It had been over two weeks since they pulled him aboard the ship. He had lost even more weight, which was terrifying as he did not have a lot to spare. He was ghostly pale and they often thought that he looked like a corpse, though no one would say it out loud. Their hope was almost non-existent; so on the days that followed the relocation of extra animals they did not notice that Alessandro's fever had broken and he was steadily on the mend.

Chiara received the shock of her life when she went down to collect eggs one day and saw a man standing with a white bird in his hand, a twinkle in his eye and a loud hunger in his gut.

She suppressed a scream and ran to see if it really was Alessandro. To ensure she was not seeing a ghost, she traced his face with her index finger and touched his hair, which was riddled with dry sweat. He was in desperate need of a wash but he was alive and awake.

As his stomach groaned Alessandro asked for a large plate of whatever they had. Chiara laughed and walked away shaking her head in disbelief.

She returned forty-five minutes later with Dylan in tow. In her hand were some partially cooked eggs and a bright pink fish.

"What no steak?" Alessandro laughed.

Chiara looked as though she would strike him for that remark, but she just about resisted. She smiled a weak smile that held a lot of cautious hope.

"Tell me everything you know about Troy and his plans. Where are they heading? Where are they now? How long has passed?"

"I know this is frustrating Alessandro," Dylan said as he collected eggs from the cages, "But we don't have time to explain anything yet. I will send Artur and Chiara in tonight. They will explain as much as possible. Chiara you go and rest now and take up the evening shift."

Chiara departed and left the two men alone to converse. Though not without a lingering stare at the living, semi - energetic Alessandro.

"You mean night has not yet fallen? I have not seen a ray of light enter this room, but the lantern in your hand."

"You had to be concealed. What would be the point in letting the sun touch your skin when you are forbidden to share air with the others on this ship?"

Alessandro could not protest. If he could see out, people could see in and they were not in a position to risk that.

"I'm glad you're awake. I don't know what I would have done with your body, had you died."

"I am confident that you would have thought of something." Dylan was not the type of man to talk about sentimentalities. He was overcome with relief and gratitude to the Gods for sparing Alessandro's life, but it was, in his mind at least, a weakness to show emotion. So with that in mind, he smiled at Alessandro patted his shoulder and without another word left leaving Alessandro alone once again with only the animals and his thoughts.

No one appeared that night or the following other than a hasty Andrew throwing in some stale bread. In fact, it was almost a week, by Alessandro's guess, before anyone came to speak to him. They had had another games tournament and Alessandro had listened to their jovial banter from his seclusion. He longed for some human company and on several occasions had to stop himself from leaving the room. Someone must have come up with the challenge of entering the haunted room without a lantern as the door often opened part of the way and closed quite fast. One person did eventually enter and Alessandro was forced to hide. The person did not stay long as Dylan was close on his tail and scolded him for disturbing the animals.

"If they get too stressed they die you fool. It's hard enough keeping them alive. Now move along to your next game!" Dylan sounded like a father disciplining his child. That brought back many memories for Alessandro and he chuckled quietly to himself.

The next man who walked through the door was not far from twenty years. He smiled and said,

"I do not believe I have ever spoken to you without a horse between us."

Alessandro's continued confinement and lack of human contact had made him irritable and he wanted to snap at Artur and demand answers to his questions, but when he came in with a big smile and open gestures Alessandro's anger subsided slightly.

"I am happy to have you as a friend, though I must admit I regret now not getting better acquainted with you."

"Worry not. You were much more sociable than others!" Artur said this with a bitter air in his tone as though remembering an unpleasant interaction.

"Tell me what you know. Do not hide a thing," enough pleasantries Alessandro thought. Time to get to work!

"I do not know much but I will tell you that, which I do. Troy is after a boy with a unique gift."

Alessandro listened intently, craving as much information as could be provided.

"It is said the boy can visit a man's dream. Twist his thoughts while they are resting. Make them reveal knowledge to him he could not have otherwise obtained. He is said to have an overwhelming hatred for you!"

"That is a heavy burden on my thoughts. Do you know the reason?" Of course, there were many reasons why someone would hate Alessandro, even before the war, but he needed specific information about this boy.

"He believes you caused the death of his mother,"

"I would wish no harm to come to any woman!"

"Be that as it may, the boy is young. Perhaps nine, ten at most and no longer has a mother to care for him."

A picture flooded Alessandro's vision, a boy with one piercing orange eye and a cold calculating blue one beside it, bloodshot and filled with anger.

"This boy, are his features unique?"

"He has the eyes of both a demon and a guardian."

Alessandro began pacing in a circle. He was not safe, even in his dreams. What would he do if Troy found this boy? What if the boy went to find Troy? He and his men would be found. What would happen to them if Troy discovered that he, Alessandro, was aboard one of Troy's own ships? This was a major problem and he needed some guidance, but from who? Who would know how to protect a man's subconscious?

"When do we make port?" Alessandro escaped himself only to find that no one accompanied him. He had failed to notice his comrade's departure.

He continued to pace and think and worry and fret and run his fingers through his hair and get exceptionally irritated when he was restricted by tangles.

He had to get out. He needed to breathe. He needed to see something other than gloom. Surely, just a few minutes would do no harm.

He crept along to the doorway and opened it a crack. There were voices not far away. Alessandro did not recognise them and was on the verge of coming to his senses and retreating to the safety of his jail, when he realised what they were saying.

"I am relieved the sea is calm. We are too far out to attract attention. Surely tonight, I can rest easy."

"Who is on duty tonight?"

"Chiara is on the deck, Dylan is on the wheel and Adam is in the nest."

"I am thankful to escape tonight; my joints are aching. Though I wouldn't mind if Chiara came and rubbed my back for me" The man laughed.

"Chiara? Gods that woman never smiles. It would be like getting a massage from the Goddess of Death."

"But what a way to die; She's a beauty, smile or no smile,"

"You have gone too long without a woman's touch my friend." The men continued their banter as they went to their cabin to sleep.

Alessandro waited for perhaps an hour or so. He listened to the sound of shuffling feet and tired prayers of thanks for the treat of a full rest. The ship was rocking gently, which would help a sailor sleep deeply. He tiptoed through the ship and up three flights of stairs until finally, he felt the wonderful sensation of a gentle breeze massaging his skin and whispering in his ears.

The sky was clear and bright. The arms of light that extended from the moon seemed to make the whites of the waves glow. They hit the dirty wooden panels of the aging ship. The illuminating stars and mesmerizing waves made the ships beauty, pale. It wasn't a new ship but it was a lot better than what most people were burdened with.

He breathed deeply. The air had a strong taste of salt and the cold chipped away at the back of his throat the entire way down to his lungs. The joy of cool freshness made his blood tingle.

He was only made aware of how relaxed he had allowed himself to become when he felt a hand grasp his shoulder and squeeze it firmly. Although he was startled, he was not in any immediate danger. The hand belonged to a frowning Chiara.

"You really shouldn't be here," she was looking him up and down still not completely convinced that he had woken up.

"I just needed to see the stars. I was careful."

Her anger subsided, though only mildly. She joined him looking out to the calm ocean currents. They were silent for a while, just dreaming.

"We had a dragon attack not long after we pulled you aboard," she spoke as though this was not that much of a problem.

Alessandro on the other hand was struck with fear, not just personal fear, but fear for them all.

"Why would a dragon attack one of Troy's ships? Do you think Troy knows I am here?" The peaceful atmosphere was once again destroyed by negative energy.

"It was circling around us for a long time. I guess attack was the wrong word to use. It was just following, watching. We thought it might have smelt you so we covered you in blankets stained with goat manure and rotten food and moved the animals in with you. It seemed to lose interest after that. It probably thought you were dying. We all did. Dylan sorted out the dragon and it left us,"

"That was either an intelligent idea or a cruel trick that worked to your advantage," he smiled. Chiara smiled back.

He thought she looked attractive when she smiled. Her stress lines vanished and her eyes sparkled a little at the corner, but only when she smiled. A childish part of him wanted to join in the conversation with the other men, but he was not one of them. He was just one; one soul hiding amongst them, not belonging with them.

Chiara and Alessandro's mother had been close, despite the age difference. When Chiara was still classed as a child in the eyes of the wise she had a baby out of wed lock. She was perhaps three years older than Alessandro and her child was only a little younger than Saoirse. So they had spent a reasonable amount of time together. People secretly questioned whether Alessandro was the father.

He looked over at Chiara. She was looking down at the parting water, relishing the spray on her face. She wasn't smiling anymore, so looked older. Stress and war stole her outer beauty, but he hoped her inner beauty was still protected.

"Where is Saoirse?" she enquired without looking up and Alessandro sensed tears approaching.

"She," he paused, "She is dead, gone to the next world. She went peacefully, well as peacefully as one can in these times. She felt no pain, no purgatory." He looked where she was looking and they both stared. It's strange how fixing your eyes on one point and concentrating with all your might can wipe away all thought and on occasions, leave you feeling refreshed as though subconsciously you had efficiently worked out all your woes.

If you looked hard enough in the ocean you could see the fish just below the surface, as well as the occasional shark that consumed the smaller fish. Survival of the fittest and most well adapted Alessandro thought. Mer people didn't communicate with ship travellers during times of war. They and their pets were neutral to land conflicts.

"My Rosie died," Chiara interrupted Alessandro's internal philosophical debates. Again she did not look up.

Alessandro knew there was more to follow this statement, but did not know how to respond. It was certainly an ache to hear it, but not surprising. The child had been weak, always coughing and sneezing even in the warmer months.

"I was attacked, by a so called noble man and she tried to … she ... Well she tried to protect me and went into a fit. She turned so many colours and went ice cold faster than I thought possible.

She didn't cry, but her irregular breaths told Alessandro she wanted to, and probably needed to. He placed his hand on hers and made her a promise,

"It will all be over before you know it, I'm so sorry for everything. I …. I really wish I could protect you Chiara, from everything."

She looked at him. He seemed sincere. His eyes were dark green but had a blanket of concern that she appreciated.

After a suitable silence Alessandro spoke again; this time of a topic that caused him great concern.

"Troy is after a boy who can blend into your dreams."

"I know."

"How can I protect myself from him? I'm afraid of giving away your secret," he sighed and found it hard to make eye contact. He was full of shame and guilt.

"We have been discussing that." Alessandro was a little taken aback that they had discussed amongst themselves and not with him. "There is a woman who has knowledge of magic, many could only dream of. In order to get directions to where she hides, you must ask her brother. He has a stall in the city we are travelling to. He makes money off his sisters' intelligence. A con man, without much cunning, but he'll tell you how to find her, for the right price."

"Where do we dock?" Alessandro was as delighted as his pessimism would allow.

"Kernag Bay."

They talked for a while about many things including war, life before it, during it and what to expect after it.

Though before long, Chiara ordered him to return to his confinement and strongly recommended he stay there for the duration of the journey as it was only a few more days. He refused to leave without a promise that she would visit him before they docked. She promised without looking at him. He took her hands in his and asked again, "Visit me before we dock...Please."

When Alessandro was feeling especially lonely he found himself talking to the chickens, ducks and scallings. Scallings were like miniature dragons only with a scale covered head and a furry body. Their eggs were brightly coloured and beautiful to eat raw.

When he realised he was talking to animals, Alessandro had to swallow a potentially side splitting laugh. He thought of telling Saoirse but then remembered that she was as good as dead. He had sent her to the world after this. She hadn't died as such, but you can't return from the afterlife easily.

His thoughts grew darker and more irrational until eventually he drifted into a terrible sleep. It had been four days since he saw or felt open space and no one had come to visit him. He fed himself from the eggs but was growing tired of the taste.

Chapter Five

He was shaken awake after a long, uncomfortable rest but was instantly cheered by a wonderful female face.

"I had feared you wouldn't visit." He allowed himself a half smile when he looked at Chiara but it soon disappeared.

"We have arrived at Kernag Bay," her face was expressionless, "Leave here in half an hour and don't dally. Almost everyone is off the ship. Those that remain are sorting through the remaining stock."

"So you're not here to give me a pep talk or wish me luck," Alessandro tried to lighten the mood but she was having none of it. She dropped some clothes by his feet and glared at him as though he had struck her and turned without responding and left. He watched her as she strode away, thinking to himself that women were strange and muttering that women used to get into trouble to catch a glimpse of him undressing; though even he had to admit he wasn't an inviting sight to look at these days.

He covered up well. The clothes he wore were 'borrowed' from a crew member. They were shabby but light. He had a hooded cloak that he had to wear to conceal his identity encase any one recognized him. The weather was warm and he felt strange, surly it would make him stand out more. It would be obvious that he was a wanted man.

Leaving the ship proved not to be a problem. It was deserted. The majority of the crew had left to find a temporary partner or make deals for supplies. Dylan was waiting for him on the deck. It was only when Alessandro saw the solitary figure deep in thought and smoking a pipe, sitting on one of the smaller row boats that he realized how little they had spoken throughout the entire trip. He stepped up to him and waited for him to notice he was there. Dylan looked up, took a deep puff and began,

"We can't dock for more than ten days. If you are not back in time we will be forced to leave and not return for three months, providing everything goes to plan. The man you seek is not hard to find. He hangs around Main Street, selling useless protection symbols and telling people words to curses that would never work. He goes by the name of Helper. Don't think it's his real name. It doesn't matter, I suppose. Well, I hope he's a help and God willing his sister is near and you will return in time." He held out a scarred hand and Alessandro shook it.

Alessandro couldn't help but think that something was bothering Dylan. There was darkness around his eyes and his shadow seemed to behave in an odd way. He was going to leave without saying a word, as he knew how Dylan hated softness but he couldn't.

"Dylan? Is something wrong? There's a difference to you that I cannot place and Chiara seems to be in foul form with me. Have I done something?"

"It is nothing that concerns you. I am at peace with my lot,"

"At peace? Dylan, are you dying? Did something happen while I was in seclusion? When that door was closed I couldn't hear a thing. Did you cast a spell? I must know if I will see you again my friend!"

"Alessandro you fool. Why do you ask for information that you do not truly desire?" Alessandro could have been mistaken but he thought that he saw tears in his friends' eyes.

"I do desire it! Tell me your woes before I embark on this quest." He was determined to learn the facts.

Dylan sighed, "If you must know there was another dragon attack a few days ago. It threw a flame at us and I had to create a portal. The portal is hidden above the ocean I cannot close it. I do not know how unless someone goes through it."

"There is something else though is there not?" Alessandro was always a suspicious kind of person.

"I got the math wrong. My soul is being unravelled I can feel it. If you do not make it back in ten days, I fear I will be gone."

"Dylan surely there is something we can do? I can't leave you to seize to exist! You are my friend, one of my few allies!" He was distraught but held himself together.

"In the centuries that we have known of these effects we have not found a way to stop it. You have a job to do and you need to do it. Go, succeed or my death will be in vain." He looked away from Alessandro and out towards the ocean.

With a final look at the peeling paint on the row boats, the rising pipe smoke and the odd shadow created by Dylan's large frame, Alessandro left, wishing he could have spoken to Chiara once more, before he left. He was so distracted he did not notice his own shadow flicker oddly.

As he walked further inland the smell of urine became stronger and mixed with sweat dampened clothes, dead rats and the bodies of unconscious, booze ridden men. Not to mention an excessive amount of animal droppings. It was a nauseous combination. Though compared to the rotting flesh in Gandros it was like a breath from the clouds themselves.

People of different heights were pushing past each other. A few had hidden their faces as Alessandro had done; they stayed at the edges of the street. He suspected that many of them were mutilated in some way. It gave him hope; he thought perhaps he wouldn't stand out as much as he first suspected.

There were buildings on either side of the street. Many of them were boarded up and looked empty, even if they weren't. Others had scantily dressed women hanging from the windows calling to the people on the street who looked like they might want to part with some money others had attractive men leaning against doorways trying to make contact with potential customers. The buildings with the most people were the ale houses. Men and women sang and fought and drank around these establishments. There were also many carts along the side of the street. Some of these carts sold meat, some almost fresh fruit and vegetables others talismans and second hand clothes.

As Dylan had explained Helper was not hard to find. His promises resounded around the crowded roads.

"Protect yourself from dragons. Guaranteed to repel the fatal flames."

Alessandro lurked somewhere between the various shadows. Out far enough from the large buildings to be noticed but hidden enough to, hopefully, remain inconspicuous.

He slowed as he neared the cart laden with amulets and ointments. He watched as the tiny man went straight up to a woman with a young child. He had a limp in his left leg; his eye was framed with a vibrant bruise, noticeable even through the mountain of dirt. He was bald and did not have a hint of a beard. He obviously wasn't hygiene conscious, so presumably he couldn't grow hair.

"You wouldn't want your child to be put in any unnecessary danger now, would you? This ointment is guaranteed to heal burnt flesh."

"What about this? Can it heal this? Your last miracle rotted my skin instead of curing old age!" The woman pulled away her scarf to reveal a putrid green peeling neck. The smell released was toxic. She stormed off looking utterly outraged.

"I have just the thing for that," he called after her, "Ten percent off to show my sorrow." She was gone without a second glance.

Alessandro crept up behind him and lent confidently against his cart. His hood remained over his eyes and his scarf stayed over his mouth. He did not want Helper to recognise him, or remember him encase they crossed paths again in the future.

"Some people never appreciate a bargain," he knew he had to choose his words carefully.

If Helper was surprised to see him standing there, he hid it well. He turned and looked at Alessandro. Trying to assess what he could sell him and how much money he could squeeze out of him.

"I believe you can assist me in my search," as he said this he dropped a bag of shinning gems in front of the middle aged serpent.

Helper's bland expression was instantly transformed into a greedy grin. He looked intently as the stones glimmered in what little light there was. He reached for the bag, but Alessandro grabbed the leather pouch and pulled the string tight. He tied the bag to his belt and hid it beneath his cloak. He lifted his head enough to check and see if he had Helper's attention. He was looking longingly at his belt. His mouth watered at the prospect of wealth. His hands began to sweat and he rubbed them together. Alessandro waited for him to respond watching his every move, planning his next words.

"I always aim to aid the traveller. What do you need? I have a cure for most ailments. Instant new face if you're in need to blend in and hide at the same time."

Alessandro had to admit the man was committed. He saw his victims and played on what he knew they needed or wanted.

"My interests lie with your kin, not with your work." He showed enough of his face now to give what he hoped was a calming smile.

"I have no kin. I am a loner. No blood connections."

Alessandro moved his cloak to reveal the bulging pouch.

"Now I know you are lying to me. Perhaps your memory is fading. I require your sisters' skill and I mean her no harm." He doubted whether Helper would care if he said he wanted her head on a platter, for a price.

Helper was trying desperately to see more of Alessandro's face, an action that was not authorized. He instantly covered himself again.

"Do I know you sir?" Alessandro continued to grin. Helper's dirty hands twitched and his tiny eyes kept darting to the pile of precious stones.

"You know I might know who you are searching for," he was almost drooling now.

"Oh? Memory is a strange thing." Alessandro cupped the prize in his hand showing how full it was. It seemed very natural and Helper was unaware he was being played.

"Yes, yes. Three days ride from here. I have a relative of sorts."

He seemed to be hoping that Alessandro would give him the bag, so to keep his attention Alessandro began to untie the knot again, but very slowly. Part of him enjoyed the tease.

"Ride at a jog through the woodland just East of here that will take half a day. Most of the trees have been cut. Then travel along the water's edge until you pass a smooth brightly coloured rock. Turn left at that and ride until another forest begins. Walk on the outside, do not pass the roots. When you feel like you want to rest keep going, not far after that, you will see a large python wrapped around a tree. It's dead but has yellow markings on its grey body. Call her name and set up camp. If she wants to talk she will come," he held out his hands expectantly.

"Her name?" Alessandro asked.

Helper looked confused.

"What is your sisters' name?" having to repeat simple questions frustrated him. He despised un-nurtured minds.

"Healer."

"Where do you recommend I buy a good horse?"

"Well I don't know, do I?" He was impatient now and didn't like to be teased or looked down on by an overconfident pompous stranger.

Alessandro opened his bag, took out a stone, flicked it in Helper's direction and walked away.

"Thanks," he called, feeling rather proud of himself and not at all guilty. Criminals like Helper deserve no sympathy nor do they deserve a king's treasure for some directions.

"What about the rest?" Helper was outraged at such deceit not conceived by himself.

"I'm sure that's enough for some directions, after all you aim to help the traveller."

Alessandro had not long left the view of Helper's stall when five large men circled him. They looked like they had had so many bangs to the head they wouldn't even understand the word intelligence; they had large round faces, small black eyes, and a completely blank expression. They were carrying large pieces of wood and waving them threateningly.

"We don't like thieves in our city." It was a slow deep drawl.

Alessandro thought it was hardly accurate to call this small port a city.

"I am no thief." He made to step forward but was pushed back. His arms were caught and held behind his back by the largest of the men. He felt his muscles twitch as though screaming in Morse code that bones do not bend and joints have limits. He tried to wriggle free and earned himself a heavy thud in the stomach. He tried to kick out at the blonde haired Neanderthal who was nearest to him.

"Helper pays a good wage to make sure no one steals from him. He said you stole a leather pouch."

He was about to protest but a blow from the right made his jaw dislocate. He received a large painful attack to the head with several hits in quick succession.

He saw a spot of darkness that grew larger and soon possessed his entire view. His head felt very light as though it wanted to escape from his heavy bruised body, and with the help of a final blow he went out like a camp fire in a hurricane.

Chapter Six

"My daughter is fourteen years old, you drunken piece of filth!" Alessandro could smell his assailant before he could see him. He sounded furious and out for blood.

"I'm sixteen; father and I don't even know who he is." A young female voice retorted with obvious distain.

"You are trying to tell me that a naked man just happened to fall asleep under your window and you haven't a clue how he got there." The man's anger was rising rapidly.

"Yes." The girl said with an arrogance that made even Alessandro roll his eyes. He was starting to become conscious.

"We live three miles from anyone, in any direction."

Three miles from anywhere, thought Alessandro. He was barely awake and after listening to the voices above him, he guessed he was in a lot of trouble even if he didn't know exactly why.

His head felt as though he was still being struck, though now the large men were hitting him from the inside. He felt blood running down from his ear. He half opened his eyes and realised that he could lift them no more than that. One eye was exceptionally swollen and the other had a cut where his eyebrow used to be.

Then Alessandro's body was given another huge shock. His muscles tensed and he gasped for air. He was soaked through to the bone with an overwhelming amount of ice cold water. It reminded him of his swim to the ship. He shot to his knees, still gasping. He lifted his head toward his attacker and as he did so, his neck cracked with every degree of turn.

The most recent attack was from a tall thin farmer who seemed to be wearing a very bad wig and a thick false beard. His fake hair was a slightly duller shade of ginger from Thalious. His eyes were a series of blue swirls. Alessandro wondered how many people he would inadvertently anger, before he even revealed himself.

The man towered over Alessandro grinning with the few teeth he had left. His breath smelt as though he had swallowed a dead, decaying rat and it had been lodged in his throat for several months.

"Dahlia! You stay here. I'll fetch the horses and the weapons. We'll hunt him in the woods and skin him alive. You, boy. You have a chance to escape. No one has ever got away from me. So mark my words, you will regret your journey here." He ran off with a slight thrill in his step. He seemed to enjoy the opportunity to hunt terrified men.

What in the world was happening now? Alessandro was obviously concussed but managed to scramble to his feet. He grabbed the girl's shoulders and hastily asked,

"Which way to Kernag Bay?" He was shaking her harsher than he intended.

She pointed east, toward another woodland area. Alessandro hobbled away, gaining pace as he grew accustomed to his pain.

"Don't hide up a tree," she called, "Or in a cave, and don't try to hide underground, he knows all those spots; that's how the others were caught. I'll catch up soon. Watch out for the savages." She was giggling like a child preparing for the fair.

Despite the danger, the main thought in Alessandro's head was these people are insane. Were there always this many crazy people in the world or has the war turned them?

So, not for the first time his feet took control. They seemed to think for him, his bare feet were guiding him through the rough paths, with the many obstacles hidden from the naked eye. These threats were more than just rabbit holes and tree roots. They were manmade traps, holes covered with weak branches, trip vines attached to tethered branches that were altered with strong spikes that could pierce the flesh and cause irreparable damage. Alessandro with his sharp vision could see a lot of the traps but he didn't know if he could see them all. The old man was a skilled hunter. If it wasn't for the adrenaline pumping through his body and making him ultra-alert Alessandro was sure he would have fallen prey to the traps.

Pumped with panic and driven by desire to survive (or at least escape torture), Alessandro listened. He had always thought of that as his best trait. Every flutter was like the beating of a Lambeg drum, every trickle was a roaring waterfall.

As he listened, he tuned into the sound of a river eroding rocks, a loud rushing eating away at the soil on its fast track. There was a distinct noise as earth crumbled to the power of the water. The pebbles rattled as they were crashing into each other in their uncontrolled haste. The splash and deafening pause, then another splash as fish jumped into the air and made a brief contact with a world they could neither survive in, nor understand.

Alessandro made his way towards the sound. All rivers lead to the ocean. He needed to get to the ocean and find his way to the one person he knew of that could help him, if she so desired.

He ducked beneath branches and toed around suspicious mounds of dirt. He suppressed vomit at the sight of a wild dog feasting on a human head with one eye still remaining, hanging out of the socket until a brave bird swooped down and scooped it into its beak, only to be snatched a second later and consumed by another starved canine.

Alessandro held his breath and gradually made his way to the river. The rocks were covered in moss and a short distance upstream, a horse lay flat out, lapping at the water, unable to reach. Foam was visible from the side of its jaw. Its eyes were black, lost in the chasm of pre death fear.

He heard sounds from both sides of the river. Both were a mixture of pounding hooves and human discussion. Behind him, were the crazed man and his daughter. In front of him was a tribe of some kind. Angry chants echoed through their half of the dense dungeon.

With all the stealth he could muster, Alessandro slipped into the water and crouched beneath an overhang of unstable earth. He held his breath and ignored the cold, not with ease.

When the two sides became visible to each other, it was clear that conflict was inevitable. What appeared to be the leader of the large group brought his stead to the front of the herd. Neither savage nor equine wore armour. The face of the leader was gut wrenching. It was covered in what appeared to be a giant scab. It had mud brown plates of tree bark instead of human skin and between the cracks of bark were vivid veins of purple and red. On its neck area was a cream and green puss filled sack that inflated and deflated with every breath.

A long twisting finger that resembled the twig of a tree extended and pointed towards the dying horse. It stretched and stroked the animal as though to sooth it, then plunged with an ear ringing, eagle screech into the horse's heart and pulled out a blue throbbing organ. As Alessandro watched it miraculously harden into a crystal. It was a beautiful blue gem that seemed to glow from within itself. The finger then reached to the horses' eyes and closed the lids, leaving it thoroughly lifeless and yet at peace.

The savage pointed now at the father and spoke in a voice that seemed to be full of the power and force of every conscious creature.

"You! And your poisons and your traps are destroying our way of life. We allowed you to stay here because you and your child had no place to go. We believed you would respect us. You must leave now or die now. Make your choice!"

Alessandro could not see the demon in their eyes but he felt a presence that paralysed him. An invisible force that seemed to tell him 'I know you are here and you are in just as much danger.'

"You have no right over these lands and no power over me! How dare you think of threatening me? Do you know who I am?"

"You are a monster that was disowned by his people and threw himself onto our mercy. You are a bringer of evil, whose magic left him after he turned. You are less than human and now you are less than life!"

With none of the gentleness that the horse was given, the wooden spear plunged deep into his chest, blood dripped from the wound. His hands fell to his side and dropped the bow and arrow he barely had time to raise. Once again an organ was removed. Alessandro had expected it to be black, completely dark and hideous. It was not. He was flabbergasted to see that it was a mixture of colours. It was black, purple, blue, brown and green. Mostly dark but it edited as it was becoming solid, colours constantly changing. It was almost as mesmerising as the portal through which he had lost his sister.

When the stone was formed into a solid, yet brittle state it was raised into the air and thrust onto the surface of a moss blanketed rock. It shattered, fragments flying everywhere, a man's soul briefly trapped and then destroyed.

The girl screamed and turned her mount to ride away. The fathers' horse was distressed. It was aware that its master had left the world and it could sense the same presence that was making Alessandro's bones shiver. It reared up showing its chipped hooves, starved sides and beaten underbelly. Its eyes were a frenzy of confusion.

"You are a betrayer and you allowed that man to be your master. You are just as much to blame as he is; so, I curse you with knowledge so that you may relive the anguish and pain that you are much to blame for." He wrapped his branch like hand around the horse's head and made him stare at the carcass that was slowly beginning to shift with the current of the water.

The horse made a quick movement and tried to break free. Alessandro seized his moment and jumped from his concealed spot. He leapt onto the horse and drew the sword that was sheathed and tied on the saddle and sliced through the limb it was struggling against. He had expected the arm to cut like wood, but beneath the bark was muscle tissue and arteries.

He took no time to explore its anatomy but spun around and kicked the horse into an unsteady canter. A blast of light came from behind them and temporarily erased the area in front of them. They stumbled but remained unharmed.

A scream travelled through the air and dominated all other sounds. It was either Alessandro or the horse (Alessandro was not sure at this point), that found the girl. She had fallen victim to one of her father's traps, a spike had been driven through her leg and into her horse's ribs. She couldn't pull it out and as her horse moved it merely ripped her leg open further. She tried to calm the stead hoping if it was still, she would be able to think of a solution but its natural instinct was to flee from pain.

Alessandro's stolen dappled grey steed called out and the other stood with its ears pricked in recognition of its partners call. The girl screamed hysterically, which did not help the dark bay animal beneath her.

Alessandro examined the injury, much to the distaste of the patient. He tried to pull at the spike, but he did not have the strength. He considered cutting it off and dealing with it later, but was concerned about time and splinters he wanted to flee from this place as fast as possible. It was only when he looked at the leather reins hanging over the wood and the noble head reaching down, that he had the idea to use the horse to pull it backwards. It seemed eager to help.

He tied the reins around the trap and asked his unnamed companion to back up, pulling the trap away from its guilty victims. When they were free Alessandro had to holler at them to move, they appeared to be in a state of shock. They had barely moved from harm's way when the straps broke and the weapon flew forward for a fresh attack.

Alessandro looked over at the child that would have killed him, just as her eyes rolled to the back of her head and she slumped sideways off the horse and onto the nettles that awaited her arrival.

By the time the girl awoke, Alessandro had cleaned and dressed her leg as best he could with what little supplies were available to him. He had covered his waist with the saddle cloth the horse had been supporting, and lit a well contained camp fire. He was still freezing but glad of the rest.

He had been too nervous to travel through the land at great haste, yet too frightened not to move onwards. A few times he had tried to go in one direction and the horse refused and led him in a separate direction.

He only decided to set up camp when Dahlia seemed to be waking up. Also when the dappled grey would not move no matter how much Alessandro pushed it onwards. He wanted to beat the animal but instead he decided to threaten to put it in his next stew. The animal paid him no heed and just stood licking the gash in the other steed's ribs.

Alessandro felt compelled to search for more plants to help heal the horse as well as the human. The saddle had prevented the attack from being fatal. Part of Alessandro believed it was a waste of time, but it warmed his heart to see the grey's concern. Luckily for Dahlia, Alessandro knew a spell that would expel the splinters and speed up the medicine.

There was a small amount of food in the saddle bags, which made Alessandro ashamed to think they weren't planning on taking very long to kill him. He was conflicted about helping Dahlia. On the one hand she was happy to watch him die, on the other, she was just a child and maybe she had some information he could use.

Her eyes opened accompanied by a full body groan. She smelt the food and saw her leg was bandaged. She looked around and rested her gaze on Alessandro for barely a second before she exclaimed,

73

"Who the devil do you think you are? Stealing my food, ripping my clothes and riding my horse!" She was in a full teenage rage.

"You ungrateful brat! I saved you and didn't kill you, even though you clearly had that in mind for me! Now hold your tongue, you are in no position to irritate me!"

She tried to stand but could not support her own weight and fell with a thud, dispersing dust. It was then that she realised how itchy she was all over and began to scratch uncontrollably.

Alessandro threw a pouch at her and told her to be silent and rub herself with the underside of the leaves.

She reluctantly did as she was told and crept closer to the fire. After a while she asked,

"Why were you naked outside my house?" She blushed as she asked but still had an angry scowl.

"It was not my intention, I assure you!" He did not have the energy to indulge her in conversation.

"So what did you do to aggravate Helper?" She laughed once more.

His attention was concentrated solely on her now. He took a sharp breath and spoke through gritted teeth.

"You knew! You knew and you did nothing to aid me!"

"I explained I didn't know you."

Again with that irritating overconfident tone. What a horrid child. Alessandro thought.

"You weren't very convincing, were you?" He spat at her.

"My father has just died and you want to fight with me!"

"I will be on my way soon enough, with your horse."

Dahlia glared at him and imagined what her father might have done.

"You won't get out of here alive without me. If the traps don't get you, the savages will!"

"I have placed a significant distance between myself and the savages, as for the traps, I don't believe you would be much use to me!"

He pointed with his eyes at the make shift first aid that was already leaking.

Once again, she scowled at him and was sharp in the tone of her response.

"I lost control of that old nag! It was its fault, not mine."

Alessandro simply rolled his eyes and continued to think about his route to Healer. He contemplated the likelihood of her being as much help as 'Helper'.

The attempt at rest was useless. The soil was moist but with no softness to it and it had a definite chill. Dahlia had started to talk nonstop about all the men that turned up. At first, she was confused then she spoke to the men one day before sun rise.

"They claim that Helper and my Dad had some kind of deal. You know, he wasn't always as bad as you saw him. Well I suppose he wasn't much better but he would not have been banished, had it not been for Helper. He told my Dad of a world that needed a savage leader, that this world was ready for the Hogg's to take charge and rule it again. Helper had told my Dad that the three of them, by three I mean my Dad, Helper and Helpers sister, whatever her name is, could come to this land and lay a plan in place to bring the Hoggronn Xzenny back to the rightful place of rulers. I don't know what the plan was but it obviously didn't work and because they left the sacred land that the Hogs created they were banned from returning on pain of death."

It is strange how a mind can be so distant and snap back at the sound of words that were presumed ignored. It just goes to show that the mind is constantly observing and processing.

"Pause your thoughts. Do you mean to tell me that you are a member of the Hoggronn Xzenny?"

This was unbelievable. A stroke of pure luck, as it had been with Dylan. It was a short cut to the end goal.

He needed the guidance and training they could offer. That is, if they still desire power and status. Then again, who wouldn't?

"Well I'm not entirely sure. You see I was born after he left so I personally have never been among the tribe. My Dad told me that my mother died during child birth. I'm not quite sure whether or not I believe him. You see I can remember things, like a smell. Not a particularly nice smell, but definitely feminine."

His heart dropped as fast as his blood pressure. He stood and began to re-saddle the grey. He had decided to call her Kara Passio. The name meant empty suffering and he believed it to be a fitting name. A New master deserved a new title.

"He told me all about the place though. Of course, you are given a choice. You can stay in the sheltered, hidden life or you can leave. If you go to explore, you are given three months and you are allowed back. If you stay any longer you are forbidden to return, under penalty of death. The same applies if you leave a second time. It appears rather harsh to me. I could never lead the sheltered life forever. That is why I would sneak into town when my father was intoxicated."

On and on she talked as Alessandro threw her onto Kara Passio. He was tempted to leave her but thought it best to abandon her at a house or to Helper, to prove a point. He wanted to knock some sanity into him.

"I asked him one day what happened, why did our people retreat into hiding? He told me. He claimed that people became too greedy and spoilt, they had no honour. So they, the royals, left when civil war broke out. The Queens daughter was taken and tortured and the Hoggs lost the will to fight for a dead land. They left them leaderless."

What lies Alessandro thought. What complete and utter lies.

"That was why my Dad was trying to rid the world of evil, he wanted forgiveness. Lots of people want to escape, he told me, but they stay for their families."

Smoke rose in front of them, above the tree tops. Not wild and out of control, just a small steady stream of smoke. As they neared, they discovered a cosy stone hut with a chimney oozing warmth. The sound of someone coughing up their lungs exited the small window and the gaps in the stone work.

With a light step, Alessandro crept along to a hole. A man was huddled by a fire wrapped in a frayed patchwork quilt. A woman lay fast asleep snoring occasionally. In a pile in the corner was a small stack of tattered clothes and in the only other room in the hut, Alessandro was confident he would find food. He walked back to Dahlia.

"I am going to take some clothes and food from that house and then I want you, after I have left, to beg for food and board. I cannot have you tailing me. I must make up the time I have lost." He thought of Dylan's time frame. He wanted to see his friend at least once more before he no longer existed.

He made to walk away but Dahlia's high pitched voice was retaliating once again.

"I refuse to beg from an old woman. I could be of use to you. I can fight, and lie and I deserve the opportunity to see more of the world than this forsaken forest. I demand you take me with you or I shall tell the world exactly who you are, Alessandro Slamina!"

Alessandro was forced now to take a proper look at this female incarnation of trouble. She was smiling a menacing grin that screamed 'I have the upper hand.'

It was clear that as an infant she would have had many freckles, though now they were faded and almost tanned her round cheeks. The rest of her skin was so pale it was almost see through in parts, her hair was strawberry blonde; her lips were thin and pink, though they narrowed more when she smirked. Alessandro wondered if she was wearing lipstick as the colour of her lips didn't seem to match her face. She was thin but no bones protruding. Her eyes though! Alessandro was shocked he had not noticed before. They were as her fathers had been, a series of blue movements, shades bouncing off one another, no pupils, no white, just a blue mess. However, as he watched they transformed, became more real. A pupil emerged and the blue was given boundaries. Even her skin seemed to gain a little colour. She was a seer, or at least part of her was. He was in trouble now.

"I'm right aren't I? This happens sometimes, but I'm always right. I saw right through you. I want to see Healer as well. I'm sure she can help me learn. I want so badly to learn. Please Alessandro, I must discover more of my gift. I promise you, I will return the favour!"

Of course he was aware that he had no choice. He could not have a vicious, spiteful teenager loose, knowing his plans. He made a mental note never to help young women again.

The theft of food went without a hitch. They travelled slower than Alessandro felt necessary, but then he was walking leading an injured horse. It was apparent that one would not leave the other.

The remainder of the day was uneventful and they managed to get back to Kernag Bay without any unsolvable problems. They were followed by a stray wild dog but it kept its distance, it would not survive long without a pack.

Chapter Seven

To someone who leads a sheltered life with little variety, the smallest of events can seem the most fascinating experience. To a teenage girl who has only ever seen a city in the dead of night, when only the public houses are lively, the sound of the market carts, smells from the bakery, and even the work of the butcher, stimulated a natural curiosity. Dahlia drew so much attention to them by gasping and pointing and, when Alessandro's eyes were averted, stealing from the stands as they past.

It came as a huge relief when they got away from all the activity. Alessandro knew he would not make it back in time to board the ship but he could not help remaining optimistic at the prospect of a miracle.

They stayed the night in a tumbling stable with the horses tethered nearby. The air grew mild and there were no clouds to insulate the sky. Stars flashed and the moon watched. Alessandro refused to give in to the persistent pressure his body was giving him to sleep. A few days ride from where they were and he was sure he would find a solution to sleep easy. For Dahlia's sake however he lay down and pretended to be in a comfortable slumber. He slowed is breathing and tried to meditate to recharge his cells and give his body strength. While he pretended to sleep Dahlia was able to cry without shame. She spoke to Kara Passio as though she were human. She spoke of her father and of regrets. The horse of course was silent and lay down. She wept into its sweaty matted coat until, eventually, she surrendered to her exhaustion.

With the persistence of passing time and lack of sleep eating away at Alessandro's already agitated mind, he decided the injured bay had to earn its protection. So when the sun raised enough to light their path Alessandro forced a stiff Dahlia onto the back of the mare so that they could reach their destination faster.

They exited the forest in a matter of hours and when they reached the beach, they took a rare glimpse of pleasure as they galloped along the water's edge. The hooves made a rhythmic beat in the soft sand. The spray of the water cooled and refreshed them. Alessandro even managed a smile at the reminder of the taste of freedom. He inhaled the salty air and rejoiced in the feeling of wind in his hair and face. His hands and legs ached but it was such a great experience to gallop flat out across the open stretch of land, they only slowed when thirst overpowered them.

He had to constantly check he was awake, his muscles ached but his head had recovered, despite appearances. Dahlia was sore but nothing was broken. He would force her to walk soon to strengthen the leg and get the circulation pumping. It might get rid of anything that could cause infection.

They rode and walked and rested often. Conversation was forced at times now that Dahlia was feeling overwhelmed and exhausted. Alessandro had to laugh with himself that after only a short time he had grown accustomed to her nonstop nattering and felt odd when she was silent. They ate maybe once or twice a day. Only what they could catch or gather, as their supplies were low.

After four days, Alessandro was beginning to believe he had been severely misinformed. Whilst he was contemplating turning back and tying Helper between two frisky stallions each wanting to pull the opposite way, Dahlia cried out in shock.

He grabbed the handle of his sword but soon realised there was no need to raise it, yet. A large, wide eyed head of a serpent had fallen from a low hanging branch. It had an illuminating yellow head with markings along its body that almost resembled words.

With a sigh of relief Alessandro dismounted and examined the snake. It felt so real, he had no idea how the body was preserved. Dahlia looked at it with rising disgust. She was horrified when Alessandro began poking around it.

"It is dead! There is no need to kill it a second time!" she spat.

"You would know all about that wouldn't you!" It was a cheap and immature remark but she was a risk to his improving mood.

When the inspection was complete Alessandro sent Dahlia to collect firewood. She seemed prepared to debate and point at her leg, but must have foreseen the response. It took her over an hour but at least there was still some light when she concluded the stick run. Alessandro placed large stones around the edge of the fire and stacked the dryer more brittle twigs on the bottom, knowing that they would ignite easier, along with some leaves.

"If you know magic why don't you use it to heal me and light a fire?" the pain in her leg was powerful, especially after her unwelcome exercise.

"For every piece of magic that is performed there must be an origin to its power. With magic you can only transfer energy to do a task. I do not have much to spare from my body and I do not know how to ensure power is not removed from my soul instead of the trees. I know the incantations; I simply lack the direction. As well as that, I believe that pain should be absorbed, it strengthens character and means you can withstand more next time you are injured. Imagine as a child you never even grazed your knee, then twenty years later you are mugged by four men. The pain will appear much more severe."

It must have made sense to her because she did not make any angry remarks. The fire was playful, it danced and crackled and jumped. The sun disappeared and the moon was hidden behind a dark cloud. There were crickets nearby making music as well as owls hooting, mice scuttling and worms digesting. Alessandro loved to listen to nature's symphony. It was calming, as though the vibrations were massaging his heart. He had not always appreciated this and at first he had despised sleeping rough, thinking it was beneath his royal stature. He now thought that if he ever had children he would set aside time to take them into the wild and show them how to survive, so they could teach their children and their children's children and so on, that way he would know that if any of his descendants got themselves into a situation like this they would be able to survive. That is if he could live through this war.

It's amazing how you can concentrate so hard on staying awake that you don't realise you have fallen asleep. You dream perhaps as though you are awake, persistent and vigilant.

There was an almost inaudible hiss, a smooth approach and a gentle winding. Alessandro did not realise he had fallen asleep and now there she was, in his dream, hanging him over the edge of a seemingly endless tunnel.

"They say you die if you fall in a dream. Do you know what happens?"

Alessandro assessed the situation. He was dangling over a possible death drop, with a snake supporting him. It was not real. It was his dream. Yet he had no control.

"Your heart starts to race, beating and pumping faster and faster. Your throat closes over. You scratch at your neck fruitlessly trying to grasp at air. Your lungs will completely depress. You twitch and shiver. You are hot while you are cold. You scream while you choke and eventually your mind shuts down, leaving you an empty shell."

He felt it all, all the temperature changes, his nerves, his throat, his lungs, an all over lack of control. He was terrified. As the last words left the snakes tongue, Alessandro's body sprang into life. As he woke he grasped at the air, feeling as though it might leave him again. From the corner of his vision he saw the 'dead' snake return to its branch and become once again lifeless.

"What is your business here?"

His heart leapt as a figure stood before him. She looked plain enough. But well adapted to woodland life. She seemed agile and strong and had a face that seemed to scream that she had definite cunning.

"I never repeat a question!"

Alessandro was secretly wondering when women became so violent and unmannerly.

"I come in search of knowledge and assistance."

"How did you find me?"

From this question Alessandro guessed she was not a seer and not a mind reader, but then how did the snake enter his dream?

"Your brother Helper gave me directions."

She spat at his feet. Her eyes narrowed and her lips moved with great exaggeration emphasising each word.

"That filth has no business with me. If you are a friend to him, you are a foe to me!" She turned and began to walk away.

"He is no friend. He needed a bribe to help and then he had me attacked and sent me to my death. It was by luck and little skill that I survived."

She turned and judged him, trying to decide if he was a waste of her time.

"Really? I enjoy a good tale. You must tell me everything about yourself and I shall judge if you deserve my help. Do not lie to me, I cannot abide lies. They are what are wrong with the world."

With the up most care to avoid mentioning Saoirse, he explained his situation. He did not lie but tried to avoid some truths. He told her of his desire to protect his sub conscious from a child intruder. He also tried to subtly comment on the bargain he was willing to strike with the Hoggron Xzenny tribe. He explained it slowly to try and read her opinion. Her face was stone.

"The Hoggron Xzenny are a neutral tribe and take no interest in the present conflict."

"With all due respect there is no time for ignorance. The world is dying and so are the traditions of every one. A few more years of this and we will have a worldwide famine. It will be irreversible. As you know famine affects everyone."

"They are protected in ways you will never understand."

"I want to understand. I want to give them status. It is my desire to right the wrongs that were committed against them. I ask for an alliance where both sides gain.

As well as that, the girl wants to know of her people and their ways, to keep her father's memory alive."

He knew that someone out there was going to punish him for using Dahlia to gain sympathy. She was asleep and looking as innocent as a new born. He thought he saw a flicker of emotion cross the woman's face, but it was gone as quickly as it came.

"I cannot return to my homeland. I will die before I set foot on our sacred boundaries."

"You know where it is. You can draw me a map. I will plead my case to your king."

"I would be guilty of treason."

"You are dead to them already. I wish to make an offer that some may wish to hear."

"I will need time to consider this." Her expression was still unreadable; therefore, a forecast of her response was impossible.

"Very well, I shall be here." She left via the nearest tree.

The trees sheltered them from the wind and provided fuel for the fire. Dahlia had made a hammock for herself as she had grown tired of the ground.

Alessandro had to sleep. He could not survive any longer without it. He had hoped that Healer would be able to do something to ease his pain but she needed time. Time was something that Alessandro didn't have. The moon was full and the clouds were once more sparse. Alessandro stared at parts of the sky until more stars appeared in the seemingly empty spaces. It was humbling to know how insignificant he really was on the grand scheme of things, but at least on this planet in this time he played a very important role.

He began to meditate but without warning drifted off to sleep once more. He dreamt of galloping along the beach in front of the castle, his home, his birth right. The sun was shining like the Gods themselves were blessing the land. His childhood horse was fresh but he was able to control it, until a large wave appeared from nowhere and destroyed the whole beach. He had to ride faster than he ever had before. He had to get to the sheltered woodland on higher ground before the wave struck him and sucked him out to the watery chasm of death. "Run Heidi! Run!" he screamed at his horse panic taking over. Then the wave disappeared and he was in dense forest. He was standing watching his horse walk away from him. He was a child. "Wait! Heidi, please don't leave me alone. I don't know where I am. Heidi! He screamed as he ran after her. No matter how fast he ran she just seemed to walk just out of reach. The trees were getting thicker and the remaining light was growing dimmer and dimmer until it was gone. He could see nothing. He was blind. It was so dark even the shadows died of starvation. Then a lantern materialized on a twisted tree. He took it but the tree trunk turned into a bleeding old face with sharp teeth and the branches grabbed at him and cut him. He needed the light to see but it meant that the tree could see him. The demon tree touched the one next to it and it woke up and partook in the attack, no hesitation. He ran and stumbled and saw his horse get caught by two trees. They wrapped their branch ropes around her and pulled her apart. He was drowning in his friends' blood and guts. The ground opened up and swallowed him. He fell faster than the roots could chase when he landed he fell through a chimney and into an empty fire. He got out and as he stood up he banged his head on pots and pans and animal skins. "Who's there," growled the voice of an old man. Alessandro tried to remain silent but it was pointless. "I haven't seen the light of day in over 50 years but I can see you clearly, Alessandro Slamina." The old man walked into the light of Alessandro's lantern and Alessandro screamed. He screamed like a petrified child. The man standing before him was himself as an old man, with no eyes, one ear, and clothed only in his own faecal matter. Alessandro fell backwards and dropped the lantern, which started a fire. The old man laughed, "You cannot escape me. I am your future Lord Slamina. We will burn together," The flames spread but the old man's face lingered in a smoky haze and his laughter echoed.

"Wake up Alessandro! Wake up!" Dahlia was sitting on Alessandros legs and had lifted his upper body and was shaking him violently with tears streaming down her face.

Alessandro shot to his feet, knocking Dahlia to the ground, both gasping for air.

"Thank you." He panted as he fell to his knees. "I think you just saved my life."

"You were making a lot of noise I had to shut you up somehow." She smiled.

They both laughed a nervous frightened laugh to relieve the tension.

When Healer returned they were eating pheasant and talking about the rules of magic. They ceased their conversation immediately.

"Conditions," she began, "They will know it was I who sent you. You must make an attempt to gain forgiveness on my behalf. Second, the child stays here with me until you ensure we will be welcome. As for protection, when and if you make it to Hoggron, you will be safe. Until then, all I can do is prevent you from sleeping. You will need a ship and crew to get there as it is a long way. As a human you do not only desire sleep, you require it. It is an essential part of your health, so I do not know how you will cope without it. You may well lose your mind. I know the boys story so I will tell you as best I can. In return I want ownership of this forest and solitude. No one must trespass on my land and no one will have power over me in it."

"I will have transport in three months and will not fail to fight for you. As for land, it will be yours and in keeping to yourself you will have no superior. I will find a way to control my wits. As for the girl her mind is her own but she shall not sail with me," he held up his hand to stifle her remarks.

"Your word on your life?"

"My word is my life!"

"Very well. Pass me a meal and I shall begin what I know of the boy's story."

Chapter Eight

To a child, their parents are immortal and God like. They don't think about it, it just is. To an infant, their worst fear is to lose their guardian to the angel of death. When a boy is raised only by his mother he would be unable to understand her absence.

It is unfortunate that in this world at this time there is a common dilemma. How do you explain murder to a child that does not even know the meaning of death?

The boy that haunts you, Alessandro, answers to the name Leo. His mother was Alicia Dovinpoir. There was nothing spectacular about the woman other than her devotion to her son. Her story is not known, neither is that of her partner. It begins sadly with her end.

The beginning takes us back maybe four years, when the war was not yet fully established. The boy was young. Not more than six years had passed since his birth. He had been sent on an errand by his mother. The task was simple, go to the land lord and pay the rent. It was one of the first he was allowed to do on his own.

The weather was not exceptional. It was before mid-day, warm with a cool breeze. It was a short walk from his small rented cottage to the substantially larger estate of the land owner. His mother had instructed him to give the money only to the master of the house.

Walking along the front gate on his way to the less sophisticated entrance at the rear, Leo slowed his walk to a dawdle, dragging his bare feet along the dry, dusty ground. The gates were large and arched, but open at the time.

The grass beyond the fence seemed to be an entirely different shade of green. The house was originally a six bedroom, two story building, though it had been expanded over the years. Stables were built as were two wings on either side of the house and a court yard. As the house expanded so did the land around it. The owner took charge of everything around him and eventually ownership was granted to him. The scenery screamed of the family's wealth.

Leo stood at the kitchen doorway. No one paid attention to him and he didn't want to upset what was obviously a well organised routine. The smell of food made Leo's mouth water. He wasn't starved, but wasn't privileged with a great variety.

"Dallvry! Make yourself useful and move that boy, a kitchen is no place for idle hands," the chef seemed to be angry. If she had asked, Leo would gladly have moved, he just didn't know where to.

The man that approached was clean shaven, tall and dressed quite smart. He wore a green cloak and his shoes were a soft brown leather. His hair was shoulder length and had a stylish wave. It was the same gentle brown as his foot wear. He suited the kitchen but it obviously wasn't his field of work. All the birds were in cages, all the meat and cheeses separated, the dishes were sorted into piles of dirty and clean. This was an unusual sight.

"Who are you?" The question was not aggressive but lacked any kind of warmth.

"I am to speak to the master of the house," to his great disappointment Leo's voice barely rose above a whisper.

"I am in no doubt that you are, but he is very busy. If you give me a message I shall pass it on."

"I am to give it only to the master of the house. My mother instructed me," he tried very hard not to stutter, but the man's gaze was unnerving.

"Who is your mother?"

"She is Alicia Dovinpoir."

"Ah yes the 'working woman' from the cottage. Are you here to pay the rent?"

The words 'working woman' were said in a way that implied Leo's mother was not just cleaning houses. Leo felt rage at this obvious slander of his mothers' character and her principles. He somehow managed to bare his teeth and remain calm.

"Only to the master of the house!"

An instantly dislikeable smile crossed the man's face.

"This way."

Leo was led past large satin tapestries of wars and fantasy. He stared at the items of clothing that were displayed in cases with bronze plaques beneath them. He was in awe at the detail of the life size paintings that were on the stone walls. It was hard to imagine that below such splendour all there was, was a boring grey wall. Leo wanted to touch them all, to feel the brush strokes. He had never even seen satin, let alone touch it. It was from a distant land.

They came to a halt outside a wooden door, decorated with a black metal design that covered most of the wood. Dallvry's shadow engulfed Leo's small frame.

"Lord Reybon is in this room. This is his private study room, even his own children are forbidden from entering it. If you give me the money, I will go in and give it to him."

His face was straight and his hand outstretched. His palms showed no signs of hard labour; they looked soft and well-scrubbed.

"My mother said…"

"Dear boy, look at you. You do not even have anything on your feet! How much more disrespect can you show?"

Feeling ashamed and saddened he reached into his shallow pockets and handed over the money, dropping his head to his feet. He curled his toes to try and hide his hazardous nails.

The man and the money disappeared behind the elaborate door. Leo waited in silence for someone to give him some kind of confirmation or dismissal or even a thank you. No one came for a long time. When they did he wished they hadn't.

"Who are you? Why are you trespassing in my house?"

A man dressed in bright colours and fine fabric stood in front of him. His eyes were bulging with rage and disgust. He was small and not of a muscular build.

"I... I gave my mother's rent money t to a man, Dallvry. He went t to give it t to the m master of the h-house. I'm waiting f-for a. I mean I'm t-think a-a thank you or um…." he faltered and his voice trailed away.

"I am the master of the house and I have received no payment. Dallvry has worked for me for a long time and I do not think well of little children speaking ill of his name. Who is your mother? She's that filthy woman from the cottage. Her rent has been late on too many occasions. You run home and tell her to vacate my property immediately." He raised his hand and slapped Leo across the face making him cry out in pain. It began to sting immediately. It all seemed to happen so fast. Leo was confused.

He turned around to run but stopped himself and did something that all the naughty boys did to him. He spat as close to Lord Reybons face as he could reach. He began to scream that he had been robbed and his mother was a good woman, and no one had the right to insult her.

As his screams grew louder, he drew in an audience, one of which was Dallvry. Leo ran to him and stamped on his toes trying desperately to make him confess.

Dallvry however remained silent until Lord Reybon ordered him to take Leo away and deal with him how he saw fit. This created the most daunting, chilling grin that Leo had seen so far. It made him want to vomit; the acid from his stomach burned him. His tears did nothing to ease the heat.

Leo decided at that moment that the devil had his doers and they were targeting him. Dallvry tied him up and threw him into a dark wooden cart pulled by a fifteen hand high chestnut horse. It was mildly lopsided but somehow managed to prevent itself from toppling over.

They travelled at a rapid speed for some time until the numerous bends began and they slowed to a walk. Leo couldn't see the scenery, though he guessed they were on the edge of a road with a steep drop. He began to whimper silently to himself. He did not want to anger Dallvry to the point of murder. The thought of falling such a height, limbs crashing against the boulders, muscles ripping and skin tearing on the jagged edges and if he survived to the water, the agonising last gasps for air before falling to the active sea bed.

At some point, by some kind of miracle Leo fell asleep. He was unsure if it was natural or enforced, though when he awoke he was being shoved into metal leg restraints that made it impossible to run and difficult to walk with the shortened strides.

When Leo looked up to view his surroundings he was nauseous with emotion. He could not see a single adult. There were children of varying ages but similar appearances. They were filthy, much worse than Leo himself, their skin was drawn tight across their faces making their eyes look unnatural. Their feet were bare and bleeding, their hands blistered from the excessive work load. Most of them had the same imprisoning chains around their ankles; on some they were so tight that flesh had grown around them causing further agony when movement was required. Each child had a task to complete. Some were ploughing far out in the fields. Others were sheering sheep, churning butter, mucking stalls, milking cows, or sanding and cutting wood. There were some older adolescents that were unbound and stood with a stick in their hands watching the others work. They too were thin and wore few clothes but did not look as bad as those doing the hard labour. Some of the older kids had other weapons, like whips with thorns and they beat the younger kids, even if they were doing as they were told to 'remind them to follow orders promptly'

Leo walked in a stunned daze, not noticing where he was being led until he was called to halt and kneel in respect to a man sitting in the middle of the town square on a raised platform with purple drapes around his chair to shield him from the sun. He was around forty years of age. He was not the King. Leo knew this because he had seen the king ride past him after a victorious battle not far from his home town.

"Dallvry Seich! What have you brought for me this time?" He did not rise from his seat, nor did he go through any of the formalities of greeting. He viewed Leo briefly with a familiar look of disgust.

"A boy sent to pay his mother's substantial debt. She has signed all necessary deeds to this boy over to you for a fee of any amount."

"That is a lie! My mother loves me and would never sell me. Sir, please believe me! This man robbed me and then kidnapped me. My mother will look for me! She will find me. He deserves to rot in a jail cell!"

Leo made to stand up and go closer to the man, who was pretending to be a king, to make him look into his eyes and see the truth in them.

As he did this Dallvry kicked the back of his knee and pushed his head toward the ground.

"The price will be reduced for his foul mouth. He is likely to cause trouble. Possibly more trouble than he is worth. No stones or gems, too weak to be worth a pig. I'll give you a chicken for him. God knows the chicken may last longer than him."

"Give me three and we will have a deal. I can go elsewhere if need be."

"When do you ever go elsewhere? I'll give you two chickens and some fresh water. Final offer."

Dallvry pretended to consider this offer for a while.

"That would be adequate, for the mother." They smiled at each other in the evil way that men of that kind seemed to do.

"Take him to a cell. Don't feed him until he learns some respect for his superiors!"

With the wave of one fat hand, Leo was dragged kicking and screaming past a large stone well that was decorated around its circular perimeter with long strands of dark grass. He was almost thrown down a short flight of stairs where the nail on his large toe caught on a crack and ripped from its flesh. He crashed into a rustic gate that was opened by his slave driver with an almost unrealistic squeal. He was handled roughly by a male who was not yet old enough to be classed as a young man. His strength at that time however exceeded Leo's own limitations. Leo did not hear the fake King ask Dallvry, "Is he the one we were told about?" nor did he see the nod of a reply.

Leo looked around his prison. The door was thick oak with five durable iron bars above his eye line that allowed others to climb up and taunt him. Opposite the door was another window of the same semi-circular design also with five metal bars. This was level with the cobbles of the square he had been sold on. Boys would come and yell through the gap, throw horse manure, spit and some would even urinate into his confined cell.

Leo felt dirty when he excreted his waste in the corner of his box. He had little room, no food and limited water. The smell was overpowering and made him feel light headed. He prayed for the ability to faint, to escape, no matter how briefly the continuous nausea.

After two days of being alone, and only having contact with another human when a bowl of water was slid beneath a dog flap at the base of the door, the door opened and a girl was thrown in. she stayed on all fours for several seconds before getting up and thrusting her entire weight against the door. She beat at it with her fists and spoke in a foreign tongue, aggressively and with exceptional volume that did not seem to seep from her lips but from her entire shaking body. The only reply received was laughter. It took her a long time to calm down and sink into a ball muttering to herself. It took even longer for her to be aware of Leo's presence.

He had crept slowly forward not sure whether or not to comfort this wild, frizzy haired older child. He stretched out his hand towards her shoulder; before he could touch her, she slapped it away and got to her feet. She looked as though she was about to hurt him but she paused and looked at him. Her anger melted and she knelt down beside him.

"I'm sorry," she sounded like she truly meant it, "What is your name?" her voice was sweet and almost maternal. It was a comfort.

"Leo. My name is Leo," he was timid.

"Well Leo my name is Gradsil, my friends call me Rad. How old are you Leo?"

"I have just turned six years."

"Well six-year-old Leo, may I give you a hug?" she opened her arms and Leo climbed onto her lap and into her embrace.

She too was bare foot only her toes were covered in a lot of blood, as were her fingers. Leo asked what had happened but she told him to sleep. Comforted by her smell that was exactly what he did.

When he woke Rad was asleep. Light was coming through the window, but noise was minimal, so he assumed it must still be very early morning. He wanted to wake Rad up so that he would have someone to talk to, but he correctly guessed she would not appreciate being woken.

He closed his eyes, not to sleep, but to escape. He thought of his mother. He tried desperately to picture her face, every line, every expression, every shade of her skin and how it seemed to change depending on her mood. He missed her voice, her touch, her very presence. He had never in all his life been this alone but he knew she would return to him.

As he thought of his mother, the image became more vivid, it was almost touchable. He could see the walls of his cottage, his mothers' chair. He could see his mother wrapped in the patchwork quilt she had made herself. He wanted to see her smiling, but she was crying. He went up to her in this image and put an arm around her. She looked up, eyes red with sadness, body trembling.

"My dear boy where have you been? They came and said you had an accident!"

"I'm here mum. I'm here."

"They threw me out of our home I thought you wouldn't find me. Friends of Lord Slamina are allowed to do what they like." she looked around and wailed, "Alas it is but another dream!"

Leo's grip on the image slipped from him. He did not know why he would imagine such a depressing scene when what he craved, was comfort.

Rad eventually awoke, before midday. She spoke to Leo as though they were friends. She was very tall when she stood up and looked quite mature, both in appearance and personality.

Leo learned that she had been in the prison for several years; she was unsure of her age and thought it unimportant. She had tried to run several times; she had also once tried to dig a tunnel. They punish disobedience severely and never reward good behaviour. Rad explained to Leo that if he wanted to survive he had to use the minimal amount of energy to do a job as possible. Do not waste energy - rule number one of many. Take your time but don't dawdle. Apparently this children's work house had been established seven years earlier. Some of the older children had been taken away and never seen again. The only adults she had ever witnessed were those selling youths, a couple who take them away and the one who decides what a child's life is worth.

Not long after Rad's arrival, Leo was sent to work. His jobs were mucking the stables, feeding the guard dragon and some harvesting in the fields. He had thought of his mother a lot. Sometimes, it was just memories but other times it was strange. He had no control over how it went. It was usually the same. His house, his mothers' chair, and his mother so happy to see him home safe, then always, she turns away and weeps.

On a late evening, about three weeks after his kidnapping he thought of her again. He drifted, only semi-conscious, weak with exhaustion, he saw her face. It seemed rather grey and thinner than he would have chosen to remember. Then more of a scene came to him, all of it, different shades of grey. His mother was kneeling at the side of a horse. Her hands were gripping a man's leg. Leo looked at the man. He was astride a large black war horse, sitting on a finely crafted saddle,

he was looking down at his mother, he shook his leg but she began to yell. His horse began to prance. He was dressed in expensive cloth and had many riders accompanying him. His beard was trim and his hair was dark with streaks of white entwined in his shoulder length cut. This man was the king.

"My husband, your grace. They say he is dead, but I know it in my heart that he lives. He visits my dreams. Please sir. I have always been loyal. Help me to find him."

Before she could continue, a boy of around twelve emerged from just behind the king. His horse was equally stunning, though not the same breadth. He pushed Alicia aside.

"The king has no time to look for dead husbands, perhaps you should have taken better care of him, been a better wife. Maybe he has found a better wife." He looked up at the king in search for approval.

"Well said Alessandro! Let us ride."

The horses kicked dirt over the grieving woman as she rolled around the ground in madness.

The scene then changed to a slightly more dishevelled older Alessandro riding a different horse. Leo's mother leaped out in front of him and begs, "Please help me your highness. I know you are the true heir to the kingdom please help me find my son. We can help you if only we can find him. He can help you win this war before it gets too bad. Please Sir if you would only help me. He has a gift. I'm sure he does. Or at least he will,"

"I have more to worry about than children. Go learn to be a better mother or don't have any children," Alessandro rode passed her.

Alicia fell to the ground and pulled the hair out of her head screeching, "I can't lose him too! Someone help me. I can't live with them both gone."

When Leo emerged from this day dream he went to find Rad. He hoped that she could explain to him what it was that kept happening. She seemed very knowledgeable about most things.

He found her locked in the stocks. She had tried to run again so they locked her in a wooden contraption. Her hands and head were at one end and the rest of her body the other. She could not stand straight nor could she kneel. It was agony on the back. She had an itch on her nose so was glad to see Leo.

The sun was down and most of the chores were done for the day. Most people were taking full advantage of this time to rest.

Rad agreed to listen to Leo's dilemma on the condition that he got down on all fours and supported her weight so that she could rest her neck, back and legs. If he was caught he would probably share the punishment. The benefit outweighed the risk. She was not a heavy burden.

He explained everything to her and she listened in silence. She was so quiet that Leo feared she had fallen asleep.

"What you have explained is strange, uncommon but not completely unheard of. There was a travelling man that used to visit our village. He would tell tales and sing songs and do humorous tricks, he was good. It was his livelihood. There was a story he told once about a gifted man who had unbelievable control over magic. He fell in love with a woman and then had to fight a war for the king. The woman did not believe that he would stay faithful to her and refused to give her blessing. To convince her of his unalterable love he gave her the gift of dream dropping so she could visit him in his slumber. That gift was then passed from generation to generation. Some could use it some could not, but it was always there. I always thought it was a tall tale, but it would explain a lot. Don't you think?"

The story excited Leo. It meant that he could visit his mother and give her a message. Tell her where he was.

"Did they marry after the war? Were they happy?" it seemed important to know the whole story.

"The man lost his memory in a bad fall, fell in love with another woman and married her. His old wife did not know of his memory loss and drove both him and his new wife to suicide," she was blunt and added no emotion to the cruel twist in what could have been a cheerful story.

"That's terrible!"

"That's life!"

"So if I can dream drop, it's not just my mother's dreams? Is it? Can I visit other people?"

"Like who?"

"I don't know, someone who could help us."

"No one can help us! No one wants to get involved in situations that require courage and bravery. You should go. They'll be coming to check up on me soon."

Leo left Rad and went in search of somewhere comfortable and solitary, which was surprisingly difficult. He went to the stables and found a palomino asleep in the corner stall. He crept in and rubbed her nose; she was startled but remained calm and soon fell back into a deep slumber. Leo went to the back right hand corner where the equine hid him from most angles. He closed his eyes, tempted to go straight to sleep. His muscles ached but his mind was racing. He concentrated again, on his mother first. He tried with all his might to think purely of her, and not a memory of an event involving her.

When he connected to his mother's mind, he did not emerge into a happy homely scenario. His mother was staring at a lake, there was little colour or warmth and no activity. No animals, no breeze, no sun or stars. He approached his mother but she was staring out to space.

"Mum?" he touched her hand and was over powered by a very strong chill. He could feel ice in his blood ripping open his heart.

She turned slowly and spoke with an echo.

"My Leo! My very own boy. I tried. I tried so hard. They sent me away. No one would listen. I'm so sorry my son. My son. My only child. So sorry!"

She turned away and took a step towards the eerie, still lake. On the surface as her toe touched the water a face appeared of a young boy. The eyes seemed to be the only colour, a strong green. His lips spoke the same words as before.

"No time for dead children. Maybe you should have taken better care of him!"

She burst into tears at the sound of the words. He was luring her into the water.

"Mother! I am alive. I'm alive and I love you. I am a prisoner. You were a great mum. You are a great mum. Given the choice I would have chosen you. Always. Mother!"

She kept walking and Leo followed her. He was crying now as well. He did not know what was happening but he knew it wasn't right.

"It's too late Leo. I tried. I really did. It's just too late. I have failed. I will be with you both soon."

Alessandro's words were still there growing louder and louder. Leo tried to scream above him. He was choking, he was begging. He was helpless.

From above them, a small light appeared. It grew larger and Alessandro's voice dulled to nothing, though his lips still moved. Alicia did not notice the light; she could no longer hear her sons' desperate plea for her attention. She had gone deaf to all sound but guilt, pure unadulterated, agonising guilt.

Leo fell to his knees; he could not pull his mother out of the water. He could not make her look at him. He could not stop her saying it was too late. This was a dream, nothing more. It had to be.

A figure made entirely of bright energy with black slits instead of eye sockets and an empty hole instead of a mouth; stood behind Leo and moved with a swift gliding movement in front of him.

"You cannot stay. You cannot go where she has chosen to travel. Go now, or you will be trapped!" The mouth of this creature did not move. It showed no signs of being any more than a picture. The voice seemed to speak with a tune behind its dull voice. When it was silent so was the music.

"Is this not a dream?" The light burned Leo's vision, and the truth scorched his heart.

"No it is not. You can see it, because she is in the process of passing. This is her final thoughts. You possess a great gift and you have learned it quickly. Your father spent many years perfecting the gift. It will be useful in your future, use it wisely."

Leo looked at his mother and tried to reach her. He called once more. She did not turn, nor did she stop, she even failed to cease muttering her chant of an apology.

The light filled Leo's sight and took control of his muscles throwing him out of the area he had trespassed upon.

From the very second he entered his mothers' final moments, Leo was determined to make Prince Alessandro get the punishment he deserved. He had not even taken the time to comfort Alicia, as a true leader should have done. He was responsible for the destruction of her life, and as a result, he was also responsible for the demolition of the soul Leo used to be.

It took Leo only a matter of days after his mother's death to succeed in finding Alessandro's dream. Leo concentrated as hard as he could on those eyes, those murderous eyes, the green that had hypnotised his mother.

When Leo found Alessandro he did not make himself immediately known. He stood back and watched. He wanted to learn how best to hurt him. How could he hurt a killer without a conscience?

He saw a spacious room with high ceilings, an open window that took up a third of the wall. It was divided into sections by black wood. Outside the window there were roses growing. Some of the blossoms were poking into the well decorated room.

Alessandro was on his knees. His hands were clutching an item of jewellery; his parents were dead in the bed opposite him. There was a movement by the door and standing there, arms at his sides, head and body positioned parallel to the now standing Alessandro was Alessandro's cousin Troy.

"What part did you play?" The sense of betrayal was intense.

"I did what was necessary. I will do much worse and a lot more, if need be. I will go to any length to ensure that you do not take the thrown. You are unworthy!"

"And you believe yourself to be worthy of a king! No one will follow you. You are a murderer!"

"I murder for a purpose not for the thrill of it, though I must say this did bring me much joy. I wonder how much of the truth you know. I am curious. Are you their accomplice or just a dumb, spoilt child?"

"You killed my parents after they took you in! You bastard!" Alessandro charged at Troy.

"Immodeeze!" Troy shouted and Alessandro's legs were rooted to the ground his upper half fell forward and he dropped his sword, "I've learned a lot Alez. I want to give you a chance to learn the truth and fix all the damage. The people will follow me with the knowledge I have gained. Those that don't will meet the same end as your parents. I have control of the Discuali. Alez, do you know how I did it? Of course you don't. You can hear but you don't listen, you can see but you don't understand. I am superior to you in many ways. You are going to leave this castle and this land. You should not cause me trouble. It is not wise. Oh and you will leave your sister here. I have a use for her. The Discuali will follow you until you have crossed the boarders and then they will return to me. Be a good boy won't you." Troy waved a hand and a cloud of the Discuali formed a hand and patted Alessandro on the cheek.

"You may kill me now Troy. I warn you if you harm my sister I will end your life with my bare hands,"

Troy turned his back on Alessandro and called to him, not caring if he heard or not.

"We shall see!"

Seeing Alessandro's dream or memory encouraged Leo. He discussed everything with Rad and over time, together they created a plan to escape and find Troy to aid him in his quest. Leo did not know why Rad was so eager to help him, but he was not about to question it. The plan would take time, but the chances for success were very high. He would not allow himself to fail. The child inside Leo got locked in a glass box of circumstances. His youthful innocence was slowly drowning, every step he took to get closer to destroying Alessandro, destroyed more of himself. He became someone his mother would not recognise.

Leo practiced his gift on a nightly basis. He learnt that he could change people's thoughts. He could plant ideas and implant suspicion. Leo could make people sleep derived, the longer they slept the more tired they were. They made mistakes, became easier to lead. All he had to do, was get the timing right and concentrate on a mental image of the people he was torturing. He thought of Alessandro and his spoiled sibling, Saoirse. He thought of all the followers of the royal line. He wanted them all to suffer a fate worse than death. He was determined to find them all.

Chapter Nine

Saoirse and Thalious had survived the journey through the portal. They had arrived in another world, safe from the war, safe from the flames of the dragon's breath. However, they had exchanged one blaze to another. They had landed harshly on an unstable floor; the flames licked at their surroundings. The flames were all around them but it was still a slight improvement, at least here the fire was not rampaging like a bull to a waving cloak. In this predicament, the blaze was undirected and unpredictable.

The glowing room had a strange sense of order, despite the fire. The room, as far as he could see had several desks of plain metallic design. There was a large gap, nearly the size of the wall in front of them. The glass that had filled the space was now lying shattered several storeys below. Voices could be heard encouraging the destruction of the orange tongues; they had long hoses that emitted vast amounts of foam that ate away at the danger.

Thalious knew that if he was seen, his plan would fail. Though, with Saoirse unconscious and his limited skill in both magic and medicine, he was unable to aid her. He could try magic but what if he woke her body and not her mind? He started to beg with the sleeping Saoirse, but his attempts were fruitless. As he turned her over he saw to his horror that half her face had been burned. He held back the urge to vomit, he had a job to do. His eyes darted about the sockets as he tried with all his might to think of a solution, then it came to him as fast as a bolt of lightning in the sky. He placed one of his thick dirty hands around her neck and the other around his own neck. He searched his memory for the wording of the childhood spells he could use, one of them having the effect to swap voices with people. He whispered a prayer to the god of child protection, even though there was no chance of being overheard. He cast the spell.

"Ah Breah Leig."

He then called out in Saoirse's voice begging for help until he heard the sound of an oncoming rescuer. He disconnected his grip and blended into the smoke, muttering to himself until he faded into the walls like the dying light outside.

In what could only be described as a crispy black corridor, a man around 5ft 6 could be seen. There was something extraordinary about this particular scene. Flames engulfed the door frame and lit up the view. Saoirse was laying out cold on the fragile floor. A solid pillar fell close to her almost lifeless body. The fire fighter stormed bravely into the danger zone risking his life for a complete stranger. With every step he took, he knew he could be nearing his death. He tried to extinguish the flames, but the expected outcome failed to take place. He swore a foreign word and with little thought for his own life he took three paces backwards and leapt athletically through the arms of the inferno. He stood over Saoirse with a book of questions swarming around his head. Was she dead? Will she be ok? Why am I doing this? I hope my wife knows how much I love her! He knelt beside the nameless girl and picked her up with some effort being required as he was now exhausted. He caught the smell from her scorched face. It was not something he would easily forget.

He stared wildly around the room, frantically trying not to think about all the negative outcomes. He heard the calls from outside beckoning him out, saying he hadn't much time. The doorway was blocked; he couldn't get out, not on his own. No one knew he had strayed from the others. That was such a stupid rookie mistake to make. He walked with great haste over to the window. The smoke was too thick for anyone to see. He pulled out his communicator and tried to make contact with his comrades, but to no avail.

Suddenly, from what could have been heaven for all, the fireman knew a voice echoed through the room.

"Jump!"

The man hesitated and the voice called again, stronger this time.

"Now you fool, do not fear."

He stepped to the window ledge and dreamed of passing out. All he could see was a contagious amount of smoke infecting more and more of the air. He leapt, believing he would freefall and die, expecting a long, loud whistle in his ears, but no. After a few seconds there was a crash, with a shooting pain in his legs he had landed on a fire escape. The hero had dropped the girl when he made contact with the lifesaving metal path that led to a few more years on earth. He hurried along ignoring his pain in the bid for survival. He jumped several steps at a time. When he reached the end there was a bit of a drop. He would usually hang down and stretch his body to reduce the height of the fall. He could not use that method this time as he had the girl in his arms and she was unable to help herself. He looked around and quickly spotted a solution. It was filthy, black and almost full. With Saoirse in his arms, the man jumped for the final time, straight into a large bin. The lid closed down on them and the bin rolled the moment they made contact with it. The entire experience was too much for his mortal mind to comprehend, so when the building exploded and blasted them further away he passed out, sure as the sky had been blue that he was crazy. As he slipped out of consciousness he could vaguely hear the sounds of frantic screaming and the shouting of his friends apparently unaware of his escape and considered him to be dead. He passed out before he felt the sharp piping that had been propelled by the blast; pierce both the bin and his spine.

There are few people in the world who truly understand the horror of waking up one morning and finding your whole world has been abruptly overturned. Few people are aware of the indescribable confusion that faces a person when they forget who they are. There are many ways that someone can lose themselves. Severe depression and mental instability to name a few, but when you have no memories, not even a name you are defenceless in an untamed world.

When you cry you cannot fully define the exact reason. Do you cry because you have lost yourself or your life or maybe the feeling of loneliness is too much to handle? It could also be due to fear, not of the unknown ahead but the unknown behind, the worst part of forgetting is the fear of remembering. What if you discover who you were and are ashamed of your actions? How must it feel to know you could pass your mother in the street and just walk on by? So many fears attack those with no real defence. It is true test of character.

Saoirse released a long drawn out groan. Her eyelids flickered slowly, steadily regaining consciousness. Not yet aware of her horrid twist of fate. There were many unusual sounds surrounding Saoirse as she tried to tune in her ears, Beeping, Scratching, and Pumping. The sound of stern feminine voices echoed with the circulating smells of cleanliness. Saoirse moved her hand across the soft cotton sheets she was laying on. The bustling sounds of movement drifted away as Saoirse fell into a dreamless sleep.

When she came back to a semi-wakeful state, there were only four active voices in the room, but they faded with time. Saoirse tried to open her eyes though the lids felt heavy. She attempted several times to lift the tonne weight of the thin flesh, when she finally felt them move, she was sure they were open because she received an immediate, unexpected stinging sensation. It was as though the air had turned to soldiers with tiny swords and was stabbing her unprotected eyes. The problem was that she could see nothing. Not a single speck of light.

Saoirse blinked again and still no result. She continued to do this until panic was flowing strong through her veins. She tried to recall a reason to what was happening and why. All she could remember was a face, a strong handsome face of a scared young man. She had no idea who he was. She heard his voice whisper, "Farewell." Frustration joined her panic she sat bolt upright. Terrified to the extent that she would gladly tight rope walk across a great drop to escape it. Her breathing quickened and became irregular, her untrained heart working overtime. She tried to move further. However, it was Saoirse's ill fate that she was restrained with wires and sharp needles piercing her skin. The machines began to beep at an increased rate which in turn made Saoirse's heart race faster which made the machines louder.

Her hysteria was further intensified when the bold voices advanced towards her.

"Don't be afraid, we are here to help. You are in Castle hospital. My name is Nurse Hawthorn."

She didn't know where she was. She couldn't see what was going on. She was frightened. Invisible people were pushing her down and her weak powerless body was unable to retaliate against it. Her eyes darted around in the direction of the most daunting sounds.

After another attempt to get free was made in vain, Saoirse merely fell back and cried out,

"What do you want with me?"

"Dear child, this may be difficult to hear. I will try to explain as best I can. You were in a fire, in a government building. My husband, a fire fighter, rescued you from the blaze. You were unconscious;" she paused to let this sink in. As Saoirse remained quiet, the nurse continued.

"He believes an angel called him to you," she smiled in remembrance of their first conversation after he had awoken, "He was released into my care last week. I am sorry to be the bearer of bad news but," she sighed, dealing bad news to children was just so heart-breaking, "No one from the building or surrounding area recognised you nor do they know why you would be there. There are no missing persons matching your description. The only clue remaining is a beautiful necklace. Can you please tell us who you are?"

She stopped again allowing the news to sink in. Saoirse's face was a multitude of expressions.

"Why can't I remember who I am? Why can't I see? Why didn't you just …."

Before she finished Nurse Hawthorn began again,

"We believe that the injury's you sustained in the blast have left your brain partially damaged. The parts of the brain that control sight and memory recall have been harmed. We are not yet sure if it is permanent."

Saoirse pondered over this news in silence aware that all eyes were now on her. She didn't know what to say or what to do. She was completely at a loss. Without any other options she asked.

"May I hold the necklace?"

The nurse had no objections. She walked away to retrieve the item. When she returned she reached for Saoirse's hand, which instinctively retracted. Nurse Hawthorn soothed her.

"It's ok I'm giving it to you."

Saoirse lay motionless with one hand gripping the blanket and the other holding the necklace tightly at her chest, willing it to give her a clue or some kind of aid.

"I know that you are lost and frightened, but when you are well enough I have been given permission to be your guardian, so you will be coming home with me. That is, if you have no objections. I will do all that I can to help you find your family."

At that she left the room with much quiet gossiping from her co-workers. They left Saoirse alone with her thoughts and fears. She curled up in a ball and thought of the family that wasn't looking for her and the memories she didn't have. She could not even dream because she could not remember what colours looked like or shapes. She was simply an insignificant medical statistic.

Saoirse's recovery was slow. She had no reason to rush it. She believed she would only be transferred from one lonely prison to the next. Her heart ached for so long she merely turned it to stone with her medusa mind. She gradually learnt to walk, which was as terrifying to her as walking unsupported and blindfolded on a thin thread over a fifty foot drop into a shark's open jaws would be to the average person. Every small tumble was her freefalling, and what was the result of overcoming this strenuous feat? More new sounds and circumstances for Saoirse to become aware of and adjust to, and more people who had no clue how to talk to her. People tried their best not to be disgusted by half her face; even after so many surgeries the scaring was still obvious.

When she was able to walk Saoirse was given a white stick, which in her mind was just a way of advertising her differences. It was a difficult concept to grasp. She started off with short walks in a protected area, then out into the hospital garden. The steps which followed led her to busy pedestrian packed streets full of normal people, with a normal life and normal memories to recall and laugh at whenever they chose to.

When she was ready (though Saoirse disagreed), the doctors gave permission for Mrs Hawthorn to take full parental responsibility of her. Saoirse thought that they had just had enough of her and wanted a new pet project to play with.

Saoirse followed her cane obediently, like a dog on a leash, being led by the cold emotionless concrete. She avoided where the stick made comment. Depression had taken a strong hold on Saoirse and no amount of drugs was capable of making her fight it.

She clambered roughly down several steps on the day that she was to go 'home'.

"You must be more careful Sarah!" A warning voice called from the distance.

Saoirse didn't think much of her name. She had refused to choose her own so one had been appointed to her.

She was led to a compact rusty sky blue car, and entered it as always in silence. She didn't talk much. Many people around her were being scolded for making awful remarks. Though compared to the things that Saoirse was thinking they were as harsh as a dead flea on a monkeys back. She had neither the will nor the desire to interact with reality or the people in it. They were associated with her sentence in purgatory.

The vehicle travelled for an unrecorded length of time. Each turn of the wheels intensified the volume of their silence. Thoughts were screaming in Mrs Hawthorn's head and yet the demon that suppressed the exchange of verbal thoughts remained in control. The uneasy atmosphere did not prove to be a good omen of times to come. It is strange to think that a car can protect you from a bolt of lightning, though it cannot untie the knots of bereavement and undesired change.

When the strange sensation of moving whilst sitting still ceased, Saoirse remained in a daze. The journey had been long and uncomfortable but it had meant that she was still in a transition stage. By leaving the car she was giving in to hopelessness, admitting that she was different and abandoned by her family.

Saoirse had fallen down to the depths of a place no one wanted to believe existed. Her psychiatrist said this was merely a reluctance to accept present circumstances. It was natural to try and hold onto something, to seize hold of, that which may explain who you are, and with all the new experiences that were going on she was finding it difficult to find a comfortable form of stability. "Which," he had added,

"Mrs Hawthorn is sure to provide."

She brought one heavy foot out and rested it on the callous pavement. With a deep sigh she brought the other to join it and accepted the waiting hand of Mrs Hawthorn. She stepped away from transition and firmly into the direction of change.

Mrs Hawthorn led Saoirse to a narrow gateway. She extended her hand so that it gripped the curved handle and instructed her to push down hard and mind out for the small step. As they walked up the path Saoirse listened with mild interest as the excited woman told her about the flowers that grew there and how she had worked hard to get a large variety of smells and textures. She explained how much planning was involved to fit them all into such a confined space. Saoirse didn't touch anything and she did not express the very slight elevation she felt, when she breathed in the comforting perfumed air.

The surface of the house was largely covered in ivy and the door had a cracked stain glass window of a dove flying towards the sun. The handle was made of a black plastic and had grooves so that fingers fitted perfectly.

As they walked in, Saoirse heard a scream from behind her,

"Robbie!"

"I'm fine Jasmine. Honestly. I just tried to reach a mug and fell. It was only as you were coming in. Please don't fuss."

"How can I not fuss when I come home to the love of my life lying on the floor?"

There was a lot of movement that Saoirse could not understand. There was banging, heavy breaths, metal hitting tiles and an almost hidden groan of pain. She was not sure what to do or say. She hadn't a clue what the dilemma was. She stretched her hand out to feel for something to use as support, to ensure she was not in the way. The muscles in her arm extended but did not touch anything. She then took a large step to the left desperate for support and felt a horrid burning on her fingertips. Saoirse was given the horrible thought that her finger prints were gone forever. As an automatic reaction her arm flew forward and bent towards her mouth, so as to sooth the pain, when she did this, her arm made contact with a glass and a cup of boiling tea which shattered on impact, both cutting and scalding her.

Saoirse had flashes of being in the hospital. Doctors yelling accusations,

"Why did you not give this child pain killers?"

The burning was so intense she thought her skin was melting. It felt as though the scars all over her body had re opened, like the plastic surgery and skin grafts were unsuccessful.

The instinct to run, over powered all other thoughts. Saoirse stepped and tripped over the door landing in a heap on a mat that read 'welcome.' She screamed and tried to scramble away down the mosaic path feeling the raised path border with her wrist. Her cane lay abandoned.

Mrs Hawthorn came running after her and with just as much ease as a soldier swept her up into her arms, calling to her husband to fill the sink with cold water and jogged back into the room. Saoirse was crying and looked so vulnerable. Her green eyes were covered with a slight mist so that when tears were added it was a formula to melt any one's heart.

When the agony subsided Jasmine placed Saoirse on her husband's lap and he wheeled his wheel chair into the living room, where he put on some classical music and hugged

Saoirse's shaking frame. He told her a story he hoped would make her feel better.

"I don't know if this will mean much to you but the dragon is a powerful animal. It represents strength, honour and family."

Saoirse looked up in his direction happy with the story but unable to see its relevance.

"The pendant on your necklace is a dragon, so who ever gave it to you must have believed you needed its strength and protection until the day you were reunited and that person could protect you themselves! Until then you have us."

Saoirse smiled for the first time in years and was finally able to rest a little better. It's amazing what a few perfect words can do.

When Robbie Hawthorn looked down again she was asleep. He stared at her and thought how glad he was he didn't hate her. He had never planned to hate her, but it was during his attempt to save her that he had lost the use of his legs. He was always a spiritual man, even before the fire but after hearing that voice and landing on the fire escape, his beliefs were elevated to an entirely new level.

As a violin solo began to play, Mrs Hawthorn joined them with hot chocolate. She placed one arm around her husband and just listened both to the music and the sound of his heart beating. She was so happy he was alive. It was always her belief that they were brought into the world to be together, even if they had to fight through illness, unemployment and fear.

Chapter Ten

Four years after Leo was first captured, he and Rad were walking along paths that had once been so familiar. Some were overgrown others were impassable but they were free.

"Leo we did it! Can you believe it? That rat Krag is going to be so confused. He will never figure out that it was him who forgot to lock us in. I can't believe after all these years we are free. Can you believe it Leo? Leo will you please at least act a little more excited. We are out of that hell hole!" Rad could not understand why Leo was being so quiet.

"Rad, Look around you. Where is the buzzing town life? Where are the country men in the fields? Where are the livestock? It doesn't feel right. Everything had changed. We are not free yet. We have just moved from one prison to another." Leo's words sounding like they were spoken by a wise old man but he was still a child and it hurt Rad to hear his child like voice say such things.

Rad picked him up and threw him over her bony shoulder, "You are much too young Leo to sound so negative. We are going to find Troy and with your amazing gift we will obliterate Alessandro and any of his followers. It won't take any more than six months, maximum."

"You don't understand Rad. I can't get into Alessandros dreams, I have tried for so long. The only image I have of him has been distorted by my hatred. I need to see him in person so I can get a realistic view of him. I can't go to Troy until I know I can help,"

"OK then Alessandro first, Troy after. How hard can it be to find the Prince?" she laughed, "He'll be in a big Castle surrounded by his servants who probably don't like him. He will be eating at a large table with far too much food. Honestly, it won't be that hard to find him. I'm exhausted now though. I think we should rest. There is a cave not far back."

"I don't think we should rest yet. We need horses. We are on foot they could catch up with us easily in the daylight on horseback with the hounds. Cave or no cave I think we should keep going." Once again Leo sounded too old for his years.

"I hate when a mini human like you is right. We will head towards water then. It will hide our tracks and our scent. There should be a farm house about somewhere. How far does a child slave camp need to be away from civilization?" She tried to smile to encourage Leo but after walking up the edge of a very steep drop in the middle of the night with only the moon and stars to guide them, she was stiff and sore and frightened. Rad dropped Leo on the ground and with the last of her energy ran and climbed a tree to eat the fresh apples. At least she hoped they were apples.

They passed a cross road and decided to keep going straight. The land seemed to be getting flatter and in the distance it looked as though there was the beginning of agriculture. There were fields with structured walls and fencing. The first of the fields were quite rocky and had sheep in them. Rad joked about what she would make for herself if she had the equipment and skill to make wool into clothes. Leo just thought about what they would taste like, it made him sad that he looked at an animal now and could only see its uses, not its soul. He didn't want to be like that but he had to.

They continued on to a large stone building. It was an unusual two storey house with stables attached to the main house. They climbed a wall and quietly crept round to the entrance of the stable block. Leo picked up two bridles but Rad told him one would be fine as it was hard enough to feed themselves, let alone two horses and they didn't want to leave extra tracks. Leo found a pretty pony the colour of pepper and about 14 hands high. Rad laughed and led out a powerful black mare.

"We will cover more ground with this beauty and I bet she can jump too, which could come in very handy." Just then there was a deep growl from behind Leo and a dog lunged off a wall straight at them. Rad threw the reins to Leo and grabbed a pitch fork and pierced the dog through the mouth and then again in the chest. She couldn't let it bark and wake up the occupants of the house or attack them and cause serious injury.

Leo was disgusted and vomited on the ground as the dog crawled, leaving behind a trail of blood to one of the stables.

"Come on!" Rad whispered urgently.

"We can't leave it like that. We have to put it out of its misery!"

"We don't have time!"

"I won't leave until we have done it."

"Hurry up then." Rad passed him a knife that had been sitting on a shelf and Leo went after the dog. When he got to the stable that she had crawled into, he saw why she was being so protective. She had three pups. There was also a boy about the same age as him sitting shaking in the corner. He had peed himself.

"I'm sorry but I can't let her suffer," Leo whispered as he sliced the dog's throat through thick tears.

"The ... the.... master w-w-will drown the pups," the boy stuttered, "and he will beat me." Leo looked at the boy's feet. He had no nails on his toes.

"Were you sold from Krag's work house?"

"Y-y-yes I w-w-w-was."

"Take this knife, take the pups, tack up a horse and come with us. We will drop you off at the next town. You deserve better than this."

"He will find me, he will k-k-kill me."

"We will protect you come on!"

The red door from the house to the barn opened and a large bald man stood in the doorway with red eyes that matched the door.

"What the bloody hell is going on in here! Who the hell are you? Why are you holding my horse? A booming voice bellowed as he clambered drunkenly down the few steps.

"Time to go. Leo time to go now." Rad was already on top of the horse she had added the saddle while Leo had gone to kill the dog.

"Come NOW LEO!"

Leo tried to move the boy from the spot that he was rooted. He could not get him to budge.

"Leo I can't get to you."

Leo grabbed one pup and stuffed it into his jumper as the large man came into the stable, "You killed my dog! You ungrateful little piece of....," Leo ran passed the giant of a man who seemed to be fixated on the boy as he was holding the knife. After all I've done for you; you steal from me with your little friends and kill my dog. What kind of a gig is Krag up to huh? Leo hit the man with a shovel but the beast barely flinched. He grabbed the shovel from Leo with ease and beat the boy until he was dead. Leo ran as the monster turned his attention towards him. He swiftly climbed onto a bale of wrapped hay ledge and leapt onto the back of the horse that Rad brought closer and the two of them galloped off, jumping a wall as the drunken daemon tried to clumsily give chase.

The pup had miraculously stayed inside Leo's jumper.

"How about next time you listen to me huh?" snapped Rad.

Leo remained silent. The face of the unnamed boy burned into his mind. There was so much suffering, so much fear, and so much murder.

They travelled for months seeing carnage and destruction. They tried to eat food that was growing wild but often they had to steal from people who had little more than them. Leo made sure that the pup was fed, much to Rad's annoyance.

"When she grows she will protect us. Just wait." Leo was feeling such strong guilt about the death of the boy, part of him felt that if he could keep the pup alive it would atone in some way.

The closer they got to the city, the more they realised how much the world had changed. War had destroyed the land and the people. There were bodies abandoned in ditches and dragons flying around loose. Children were crying and blood ran through the cracks in the cobbled streets.

"I guess there is more going on than we understand. We need to get information. Obviously, while we were trapped Troy and Alessandro have been busy. If we head toward the palace there might be something of Alessandros you can use to get an untainted connection to him."

They had a long journey ahead of them but they were focused and determined. Leo's hatred grew stronger with the passing of time and his gift developed into something formidable. The little boy was drowned; the weapon was born.

Chapter Eleven

Several years had passed since the eventful day in which Saoirse had been found next to the fire wrapped building, and she was none the wiser about what had brought her there. She knew as many people do when placed in strange situations that where she was, was not where she was supposed to be.

With that thought constantly on her mind, she had chosen to make little effort in the area of fitting in. If given the choice she would be more reclusive than was healthy. However, Saoirse's foster parents were determined even after such a long time. She had been enrolled in an expensive school that claimed to cater for Saoirse's not so unique situation, Saoirse was smart and coped physically well with her lack of sight.

It could have been her age or maybe just the product of her unfortunate circumstances, but Saoirse deep down always felt a presence follow her. It was different than when someone was actually standing near her because you couldn't hear breathing or movement. It was as though the air was thicker. Her psychiatrist claimed that it was mild paranoia associated with her condition and possibly a side effect of her medication. He suggested changing her to a different course of drugs.

Whenever she closed her eyes she could almost hear a distant scream, a skin shrinking plea for help. Her psychiatrist explained that it was more than likely repressed memories from the fire trying to surface to the conscious layer of her mind.

Saoirse found it hard to question him. When she was a child he had been able to comfort her with almost magical ease. She felt relaxed around him. That was why her parents had decided to use him to help Saoirse heal mentally.

When Saoirse left his office one day in the spring, she had absolutely no confidence in the new experimental drug. As she walked out, the thought crossed her mind, as it often did, about what her doctor must look like. She knew he was small with broad shoulders, she also knew that his nose was wide and quite flat, his lips were full and his eye lids were soft. She had felt awkward the first time she touched his face. She felt that she was crossing some kind of personal barrier. He told her that it was only fair and she deserved to be on level ground with any one she met.

"Good bye Dr Samnal," she called through the closing door.

"Have a nice week Sarah and don't expect too much."

She had long ago given up expecting anything. A girl in her school, someone she had grown close to, had gained her sight after a very dangerous operation. She left the school and went to socialise with other children. She visited at first but then stopped. She told her that the visits made her depressed and she wanted to move on with her life. She wasn't cruel about it, but she just couldn't bear to think about what life had been like before.

Saoirse placed her hand on the cool door frame. She felt it up and down and especially noticed the distance from the lock to her head. She realised how much taller she had grown whilst in the process of finding herself.

She sighed and stepped into the waiting room. Not even a second later came the repetitive scrapping of chairs as her foster parents rose to guide her back to the car.

"Before you ask, there was no miraculous break through, no hidden memories, and no long lost relatives, just new pills and a book written in brail for me to read."

"Would you like to talk about it?" Jasmine tried to be comforting.

"No offence mum, but you pay him a lot of money to listen and I don't see the point in talking about things I can't change!"

As soon as Saoirse was clear of his office Thalious spoke aloud the words, "She is gone," and a fuzzy image of a woman appeared.

"What news have you?" Dahlia looked stern.

"It is getting harder to control her. I do not have the power to keep away her memories indefinitely. It has been ten years. Is it not yet time to come home? She needs to be home," Thalious pleaded.

"You will do as you are told when you're told to do it. Do you understand? The time is not right yet. Do not fail us! Alessandro does not like complications. Now can you keep his sister safe? Or are you now obsolete?" Dahlia loved to assert her authority. She loved the control she had. She had come a long way since Alessandro had found her almost feral in the forest. She was important. She was a vital component to the plan and she loved it.

"I will not fail. I am as loyal now as the day I left." Thalious was affronted by her accusations. He had originally thought Alessandro would find the dream pools and communicate with him directly, but when he found this foul mouthed vulture the plans had changed. Alessandro trusted her but Thalious did not.

"You are a good man Thalious. You will be well rewarded when the time comes." At that Dahlia's image disappeared.

The drive home was never talkative. Saoirse didn't like to be rude. She loved her parents and she was grateful for all their help, but sometimes the frustration was unbearable and she had to take it out on some one.

When the car stopped, Saoirse stepped out and tripped on the kerb. Mrs Hawthorn's parallel parking was never something to be admired. There was a smashed bottle of beer on the ground and it cut the palm of her hand.

"Oh dear! Are you alright? Come on and I'll fix it for you."

"Mum, please. After all this time, there is no need to fuss about every tiny tumble. I know where the sink is, I know where the antiseptic wipes are and the plasters. I'll be fine."

They pushed through the gate and up the mosaic path, passing the strong scented flowers, which had been planted especially for Saoirse over a decade ago.

Saoirse tried to sort her most recent injury out herself but her groans brought Mrs Hawthorn running.

"Please Sarah. Let me do it. You'll need a couple of stitches. I'll leave you alone for the rest of the evening if you like."

Saoirse gave in and allowed the nurse, who now knew to have a readily available supply of first aid, to deal with her wound.

When the stitches were in, she retreated to her bedroom. The bed had been calling her name since she left it that morning. She changed into her night dress and climbed into her double bed, with her thick padded quilt and feathered pillows. She lay and listened to her breath escaping then rushing back and escaping once more. The breaths became shallow and her eyes gained weight.

As Saoirse gave no fight against the drooping of her lids, she expected once again to meet with no emotion the colourless emptiness that had plagued her all her known memory. She had given up on her search for the past; she had given in to the fact that she was a no one. For a brief while she believed that perhaps she was sent there for a reason, that maybe God had sent her there to do a task. That idea was abandoned with the shortening of life's string. She was living each day not for any purpose, just for the curiosity of age.

She drifted from conscious to unconscious much as she did in waking hours between sanity and insanity. She took some time before settling into a slumber that would not be broken for several hours.

As expected there was a depressing darkness, same as there had been for several years. Though after not but a few seconds in this state, the darkness began to swirl. Saoirse could feel a breeze. For the first time she saw shades they were still dark but after what would seem an eternity she had more than just a solid black screen blocking her from what lay behind veil.

Saoirse stepped forward stumbling slightly as she walked, unsure of her steps and dizzy from the constant rotation. She was so excited now. She could see. Maybe this was just the beginning. Perhaps this is the spark that would ignite her memory and allow her to set eyes upon the two people she cared for so dearly. Part of her was scared at what all this might mean; about the changes it could bring. What if it amounted to no more than this?

The grey and black mess began to move faster. Not just in a circular rotation now. It was much more erratic and unpredictable. New combination of colour joined it. Saoirse began to feel nauseous. She was on the verge of collapse, which is a strange sensation when you're already asleep, when everything suddenly stopped.

The scene that lay before her was the best sight that one could hope for when seeing for the first time. It was a picturesque country view. The leaves in the trees had several colours, Glorious gold's, refreshing reds, not only different shades of black but solid colours with differing degrees of intensity. She was in paradise. There was so much activity that she had never seen before. She now knew the purpose of the breeze; it was to make everything that much more beautiful. The grass was nothing as she had imagined. Its moisture added to its wondrous looks. It played joyfully with the wind she used to hate. Saoirse had always felt that the wind was there to mock her. To kick her when she was down and blow things that she could not see. The warmth of the low laying sun felt terrific, it was no longer a reminder of the fun that other people had on their holidays. Its rays made everything seem different, like the shimmering of puddles. Shadows were no longer the minions of evil; they were a beautiful phenomenon. This scene is lost on so many people, always seeing but never noticing. Dust and leaves and smells were flying and falling. Saoirse felt sure that no one had ever felt this good by looking at a dusty dirt road, with wooden fences running parallel alongside it, with grass and wheat on either side.

Saoirse had an overwhelming urge to climb onto the fence, to feel the glory of sight and height with no fear, no guidance. She wanted to experience the pressure of gravity knowing full well that there was no dark chasm waiting to swallow her up. This was so fantastic to her, but was it real?

How could she go from the still, guarded life in a small room to a restful paradise?

Saoirse bent down low to the ground and picked up a fistful of dirt and examined it closely, seeing the insects crawl across her hand. She had no idea why people would cringe at that thought. She went over to a tree and began inspecting the grooves and lines and dents and colours. Saoirse could not help but breathe in the ecstasy of the unexpected heaven.

However, as inevitable as grey hair, Saoirse's depression returned. What if this feeling never returned? Would she be forever in a search for the glory she felt at that very moment? She might waste her life looking for another glimpse of it.

In the distance, there were some buildings just about in view. Saoirse put her depressing thoughts out of her mind and set off to see if there was any kind of civilisation. She wanted to see the buildings before the already dwindling light was extinguished.

As Saoirse walked, she was making mental notes of sights to go with smells. She couldn't help but smell and touch everything; if this miracle was only temporary, it was going to leave her with the best memories of her life. She took great satisfaction in being able to see shadows lengthen, though perhaps, because of a fear of her blindness returning, Saoirse rushed inside a building before the land was in a full blanket of the shadows that had amused her.

It took her a matter of minutes, after she had entered the building in a state of not so irrational fear, before she noticed the true beauty of what stood before her. The entrance was host to numerous doors; the ceilings were as tall as an oak tree. The stairs were made of marble; the banister was smooth with a light varnish and a spiral end.

The walls were cream but with a faint hint of a light green. Saoirse was in awe at the charm the hallway possessed and was eager to explore further.

Although some would say it would be more sensible to explore the downstairs rooms first, Saoirse admired the elegance of the stairs. She was in a trance as soon as she set eyes on them. She had to evaluate each step against the one before it. Each had an individual infusion of colours. They had their own personality.

When she had reached the landing she was still in a hypnotic state. It took Saoirse a while to tune her ears but she was sure she could hear the sound of excited feminine voices. She followed the noise with intense curiosity and mild fear.

"Should I wear this?" the first excited voice asked.

"No! The colour is far too bright; you want to be subtle." Her friend giggled.

"Oh Chiara! I don't know what I'm doing! Should I be doing this? Should I be excited about doing this?"

"You love this man. You need to know if he is willing to make the same sacrifices that you are. By the end of tonight you will know one way or the other!"

"Please come to this ball with me. Your assistance is indispensable. I will be lost without you."

"Look at me Rebecca! I'm hardly the image that is proper in civilised society."

"You may have gained a little weight. I'm sure no one will talk foul of your name if you enter with me."

"I am pregnant and many people know it. I do not wish to put a mark on your name. You are a very important member of this kingdom."

"I have no say in political matters. Besides, get your secret young man to join you and clear up this entire mess."

"He no longer wishes to be seen with me, I must face facts. I am fourteen years old and my life is over. I am just fortunate that you have been so kind to me."

There was a brief unpleasant silence between the two women. Saoirse had followed the voices to a large door that was slightly ajar. She did not know if she was dreaming or if she had been transported somewhere, but Saoirse wondered if she knew these women. Were they a memory perhaps? Or were they just a dream? Who were they? Did they know her? Saoirse had become accustomed to her own compulsive enquiring.

Just as Saoirse was debating about going in or leaving she heard the sound of a young baby cry.

"My little Saoirse has at last awoken."

Saoirse felt that entering now would be cruel. What if they didn't know her and she had just broken into their house! And yet she just had to know. She opened the door and with a short hesitation walked in. She wasn't sure what she had expected but it was definitely not what happened. They did not move. Not even a flinch. Saoirse went up and waved a hand in front of their faces. Not even their eyes flashed in her direction.

Saoirse watched as the baby fell asleep in the arms of its mother wishing with all her heart that it could have been her. The women slowly faded until they were no longer visible. Could it have been some kind of memory? Or maybe they were ghosts? Or perhaps they were not and never had been alive. Maybe she made them up.

Saoirse walked along the corridor admiring works of art, touching the paint where the brush strokes had left some parts of the painting raised more than others. She loved the pictures of the people most. The majority of the men had the same pose, but some of them had a little added character, such as a sideward smile or a wink or even just a different position. It was interesting to see how the styles of clothes and hair changed after a few paintings. She seemed particularly interested in the way the colours went in and out of fashion, beards too seemed to come and go.

Some doors would open for Saoirse with ease, while others either needed some effort or would not open at all. She spent her entire dream just exploring and making mental notes. On some occasions, she would see someone, a partial image; mostly a flickering head and shoulders walk past her. She also heard voices but could not reach them before the image dispersed, if it was even there to begin with. This gift was too much for Saoirse to comprehend. What had triggered it? Would it happen again? Or was this the only time it was to happen, like some cruel tease.

Somewhere around her, or perhaps above, Saoirse heard a voice that she did recognise. The sound of it made her grip the banister tightly it was different from the others. She tried to hold on to the image, to stay where she was even just a little longer.

"It's time to get up Sarah; we have a lot to do today!"

An alarm was sounding and guided Saoirse away from the colours and half memories. The shades merged together and rapidly returned to the familiar empty darkness.

Saoirse began to yell. She could not grasp the vision and as she blinked she screamed and beat the alarm beside her bed. She ripped it from the socket and threw it across the room. Something shattered but Saoirse did not care. Her anger subsided to sadness and then transformed into fear.

By the time Mrs Hawthorn reached her, she was crying. Jasmine climbed onto the bed and rocked her until her breathes became regular.

"What is it sweet heart? Why are you so upset?" She would not loosen her grip.

"I dreamt. I saw colours. I saw faces and now it's gone!"

"Oh Sarah honey, that's a good thing. It is a very god sign. Would you like me to try and make an appointment with Dr Samnal? Maybe those tablets were a good start, though it usually takes a while for them to enter the system."

"I didn't take any tablets last night. I fell straight to sleep. Mum. It was so wonderful and now it's gone."

"If it came once, I'm sure it will come again. Come on get ready. It's your dad's birthday today. Let's go and tell him the good news."

The day wasn't terrible, though time sailed by at an agonisingly slow pace. Saoirse made her Dad breakfast in bed and they went for a trip to see Robert Hawthorn's old fire fighter colleagues. They had an early formal dinner, which for Saoirse was very uncomfortable. Even after a decade, they were still afraid to talk to her and say the wrong thing. She knew they blamed her for Roberts suffering. After the dinner, Saoirse went to see her psychiatrist.

She explained to him everything that she had seen, as best she could. She told him about the emotions it provoked within her and how a renewed fear possessed her of the darkness in which she had grown accustomed to.

"What I must say is that although it may seem like a memory, you have described a situation that is unlikely. However, it may be a collection of childhood memories from a play or television show. It is still a good sign. Enjoy the sight and try to concentrate on where you saw it and why it is important enough for you to remember. Don't get too excited and be careful not to confuse dream and reality."

Saoirse felt a little deflated as she travelled home but put on a brave face for her father's benefit. Dr Samnal advised her to take the tablets he had prescribed as it was unhealthy to just stop. After a car journey of thought, she decided that she would wait just one more night to see what would happen.

Robbie Hawthorn was a great fan of classical music and took great pride in his daughter's ability to play the piano. She knew it made him really happy and the sound and rhythm soothed Saoirse's nerves as well. She played him a birthday tune and wished her parents luck on their night out. She hugged her father and felt the pang of guilt she sometimes got at the fact that he was still in a wheel chair. The good news was that he had got some feeling back in his legs, but was not yet able to walk or stand for long periods of time. It was still so much more than anyone had honestly expected.

She waved them off and hurried straight to her bedroom. She tried desperately to fall asleep but her apprehension was too powerful. She tried deep breathing exercises and counting slowly. In the end she made herself a cup of hot chocolate, put on some music and waited for sleep to sneak up on her.

When she did drift off, it happened much the same as the previous night, only much slower. Saoirse could barely contain herself. She leapt up and down and began what she presumed was a victory dance.

This time, Saoirse ran to the same building and decided to explore the ground floors. She looked in several rooms briefly but there was so much to see. She was enticed into a room at the far end of the entrance hall. It had huge double doors and the sound of music was resounding off the walls of the corridor. The music was medium paced with a strong melody. Saoirse pushed open the door and was amazed to see a spacious room lined with tables of food, some meat, others grapes and bread, there was wine and ale, everything a high standing person could ask for. It was a marvellous feast. In the centre of the hall were more people than Saoirse had ever met, or could remember meeting. Most were dancing with enthusiastic smiles. Though a few were standing unsociably on the outskirts looking very unhappy, or nibbling on the food and engulfing large quantities of intoxicating wine and ale.

Banners and flags were proudly displayed on the walls. Dogs were sitting obediently at the top table with a small number of non-active men and women. The man and woman in the centre of the table had large false smiles but were cheering and clapping and putting on a great show.

Like the two women in the pretty peach room and the numerous semi translucent figures that walked around, no one in the room noticed Saoirse. No one cared that she walked up and listened to their conversations or admired their dress sense or even danced alongside them.

Saoirse noticed the different flags and shields. Some were simple, just colours divided by a cross. Others were more elaborate with animals and symbols. Each shield sat below a matching flag. Saoirse also noticed that some of the cloaks matched a flag in some way. So perhaps, this was a political event. She learned so many of their names and as the night went on she had timed her steps so that she could pretend they were dancing with her. The mother from the peach room was sitting in a chair at the top end of the dance floor beside a very tall man who was also in a finely decorated chair. A few times during the night both men and women had gone up to the woman and asked her to dance 'like she used to love to dance' but her husband put out his large hand and squeezed her bruised wrist, "She is too tired to dance tonight," and waved them away. The woman looked so defeated but Saoirse could still see a slight glimmer of hope.

Saoirse moved through the castle and went to the expansive gardens. With just a thought and a step she could change the seasons, so she could enjoy the same spot 4 different ways. She walked towards the private woodland that had a path made from red and white logs. Along the side of the pathway there was stone artwork, metal sculptures and wooden carvings. They were all of different designs. Then she heard angry voices just off the path, through the tall trees with the blood red bark and yellow leaves. It was dark but the night flies were illuminating both the pathway and the clearing around the two men. With every beat of their tiny wings they spread out dust light and a short trail of it followed them as they flew. They were there for when the royals or their guests wanted a moonlight walk but did not care to carry a lantern.

"You will tell me what you have discovered or you will never see your child again, do you understand me Derrick. I don't want to hurt you but I need the answers that you possess. Give them to me and you can go back to your little family on the farm behind the mountains. You helped me once before why will you not help me now. I saved your life, remember. I won't hurt anyone I just want to know if I am being made a fool of. You wouldn't want me to suffer an injustice would you Derrick?" It was the husband from the dance.

"She loves your brother Samuel. They love each other. This could be a way to right the wrong we committed all those years ago. Had we not interfered they would be together now. Let them be together," Derrick was sweating with fear and was scratching the back of his hands until he bled. He looked and sounded as though he truly wanted to atone for a past misdeed.

"The rat child, is it mine or his!"

"You have raised the child and shown such love..."

"Answer me!"

"You have only one child your highness. One is a bastard. I warned you when we began messing with her mind that some things just can't be controlled,"

"You are going into my brothers dreams and you will torture both him and his wife until they truly understand not to get in my way,"

"Sir, Theresa knew nothing of his indiscretion. She knows not where his heart truly lies and they have a son. What will happen to their son? Please don't make me do this."

"I know where you heart lies Derrick and I know the power you possess, just as you know the power I have. Go now and do as I say. Oh and Derrick don't try to kill yourself again or your family will suffer the consequences," the image of them faded and Saoirse was disgusted. What a horrible man. Some child was lucky not to have him as a father.

She continued walking the streets and woodland and entering houses until the dreaded alarm clock called her back to the reality she didn't want.

"Sarah. Sarah. Come on love it's time to get up." Oh how she hated that sound at that moment.

Chapter Twelve

As the nights rolled to weeks and the weeks ticked to months, Saoirse spent more time asleep or attempting to sleep. She did not take her tablets and often skipped meals. Her excitement about Gandros was blinding her to the fact that her health was seriously deteriorating. Her bad nutrition was a growing concern for her parents. They were at first excited at Robbie's gaining strength and Saoirse's night time sight. They had assumed it was the beginning of her memory returning, which had also been a little worrying. They feared that they would lose her to another family, now they were terrified that she was going to get very sick.

During the months of Saoirse's solitary searching, she became accustomed to the lands hidden pathways and historic monuments. She knew all the buildings, from the extravagant palace on her first visit to the smaller dwellings that had been erected in a circular pattern around the estate of the palace.

She felt most comfortable (especially after a night of parental health discussion), in a beautiful blossoming country park. The paths were lined with bright short flowers that led to different plant beds of varying design. The trees also seemed to be different from each other. Some were vertical with leaves only on the upper branches. Most had some kind of fruit that littered their roots; some trunks were blanketed with ivory or white petals. The sturdier the tree the more animals inhabited them. The sun rays trickled through the waving branches almost like rain drops. The wildlife was as oblivious to Saoirse's presence as the dancers.

Although it was a little lonely, Saoirse was not to be discouraged. She wanted to know more, wanted to see everything. She could not deny the desire to see human expressions, when communicating with her, was strong. She wanted to react to someone else's impulsive cringe or subtle smile, she wanted to know what made people's eyes shine and what made a face dull. Witnessing such things from second hand conversation was just not the same.

On one occasion, Saoirse had chosen to visit the beautiful woodlands after a particularly gruesome conversation and found that she was uneasy. She threw the fight from her mind and paddled in a refreshingly cool lake. Somehow, she could not shake the feeling of being watched. Being blind had given her the ability to know when someone enters your space. It was not the first time that Saoirse had acknowledged this almost foreboding threat but she had found ways of rationalising until the fear was practically non-existent. This time her nerves could not handle it and she called out to her stalker, half hoping for no response and partially begging for one.

"I know your there! Your time for hidden haunting is over! Show yourself, or I will be forced to take action."

Of course, Saoirse had no idea what that action might be and it took her some time to realise the response had mimicked her thoughts.

"And what action would you choose to take against an unknown assailant?" The voice was male and lined with a hint of a mocking tone.

"I can fight!" Saoirse took a step backwards away from where she presumed the voice originated. She only just managed to catch her balance as she had not realised the height differences in the floor of the lake. She was determined to at least appear confident.

"If I do not show myself, how do you intend to fight me?" he was finding it difficult to contain laughter.

"I would find a way. Now stop your mocking and show yourself!"

A tree close to Saoirse began to shake. The wind caught the seeds and blossoms that broke free and set about planting them elsewhere. A few twigs fell and bounced on the soft earth. Two pieces of fruit dropped, rolled down the gentle slope and lay idle not far from the edge of the lake. Saoirse's eyes followed their movement. When they stopped her eyes reverted back to the tree. The shock made her gasp for air and step backwards once more.

A young man stood tall, leaning confidently against the rough bark of a tree trunk. His hair was almost white, his smile showed all his teeth and he was standing in direct sunlight. His height was just short of six foot. His clothes were loose and were earthly colours. Some would say his dress was modest but his expressions gave off a strong sense of self-importance.

"Who are you? Do I know you? Why can you speak to me and nothing else can?"

"Isn't it obvious who I am?" He walked towards Saoirse and held out a hand to guide her back to dry land.

She looked at his hand with caution and before she accepted it she said, "If it was obvious, I wouldn't need to ask!"

He pulled her forward and made eye contact with her, "I'm the man of your dreams."

Saoirse had never come across a character as bold as him and thought that his attitude was entirely inappropriate.

Freeing herself from his grasp she took several steps away from him and gave him a warning snarl.

"Don't play games with me! You must be an insignificant figment of my imagination which means that I have the power to make you disappear."

This sudden comprehension gave Saoirse confidence in her speech and actions. The man couldn't be much older than she was and she was asleep so he posed no real threat.

The man laughed aloud, and then caught himself in mid snort as he stood up straight and bowed.

"I apologise for my inexcusable rudeness. My name is Leo Dovinpoir and I accidently fell into your dream whilst in search for someone else. I liked it so much I decided to visit a few more times. I beg for your forgiveness."

Saoirse looked him over. He did not seem to have entirely recovered from his fit of laughter.

"My name is Sarah Hawthorn. Your forgiveness is pending."

There was an exchange of analysing stares in which each person recorded as much detail about the other in as short a time as possible. Saoirse was intrigued by his eyes but was too afraid to look for long. She could not decide if they scared her or put her at ease. Eventually, she held out her hand.

"I'm pleased to meet you." She was still suspicious but thought it might be fun to have a companion.

"As am I. Though you must tell me how you came about the knowledge of this land. The detail is incredible." He looked around as he spoke.

"What do you mean? This is my dream. It is my sanctuary." She was not yet sure if she was willing to explain that she was blind and had no memory or any clue about the realm or world that she visited each night. "You sound as though you know of it. Does it exist? Is it where you come from?" Maybe Leo was the part of her subconscious that was going to guide her. Dr Samnal had explained that she might create someone to show her through her thoughts. She was a little curious as to why she would create a persona so unlike herself or anyone she had ever met, so antagonising and rude. Then again, perhaps that was the point.

"This place used to exist. I suppose it still does but not in this elegant and enchanting way. It is in danger of being destroyed."

This clearly affected Leo. His smile faltered and his eyes showed his shift into memory.

"What happened to kill the beauty?" She was genuinely curious.

"Death, murder, betrayal. Two power hungry men. It is a long and complicated story. No one knows all the facts and not one person is going to snoop around to find them. I might tell you what I know, but not yet."

Saoirse picked up on the same desperate desire for escape that she had felt. She realised they did have something in common after all.

"Will you tell me about the buildings and the animals? Some of them are very strange to me. You can tell me all about this land the way it is here."

"It would be my honour. Your sanctuary has become mine in recent months and I would love to reminisce. Mind you, remember all this was destroyed when I was small so my memory on all the facts is not entirely reliable."

Saoirse was a little worried that he had been in her dreams for a few months but decided to dismiss it. She walked with him and enjoyed hearing the tales of his childhood. He knew some of the political people and royal family members.

Sometimes, he would get so excited about a story he had once heard or a game he used to play, that he would run and jump like a child, do imitations and act out as much as he could about what he was trying to explain.

It soon came to be that Saoirse was going to sleep to see what else Leo could tell her. He showed her places she had not even noticed before. At first she had walked beside him hearing his stories and learning the lay of the land, then she had linked arms with him partially to stop him jumping around like some kind of bean and partially because she wanted to be closer to him. Then one day he took her hand to pull her toward a street and that was how they walked now, hand in hand where ever they went. She learnt all about him and asked many questions. There were many things he wouldn't talk about and refused to say anything too depressing. He told her it would kill him if she cried, and explained that it was their sanctuary away from hell, so they had to keep it cheerful. Leo was always there when Saoirse fell asleep. He told her it was his job to track people using their dreams and he felt like her dream was a vacation.

Saoirse soon decided that she liked the different colours in Leo's eyes. It put her at ease. She could not remember what she had ever found disturbing about them. They spent a lot of time together and grew quite close. Well as close as two people who refuse to explain everything about their past can get. They enjoyed each other's company and were both risking something to escape to Gandros. Maybe he was the man of her dreams Saoirse laughed on occasions. He was helping her to discover who she really was. He made her feel safe and she could talk to him with an ease that she had never experienced before, even if he was the most impossibly irritating person at the same time.

"I have to ask Sarah, Your world sounds so different to mine. How did you find this place? If magic does not exist in your place how is it possible that we are here together."

Saoirse wanted to say 'love conquers all and they were meant to find each other' but she thought that would sound way too ridiculous. Even if Leo wasn't just a figment of her now over active imagination it was a stupid thing to say.

"I guess we both so desperately needed freedom that we willed this sanctuary into existence. The mind is a powerful thing,"

"You don't half talk the biggest pile of dragon dung," Leo laughed as he threw the autumn leaves at Saoirse and ran off. She turned the season to a snowy winter and threw snow balls at him. He was fast and so cheeky. They both enjoyed her power over her dreams. It meant that they could enjoy their time together so much better.

After they built a few snow men she turned it back to summer again and they climbed trees. Saoirse couldn't understand how in her dream she could change the seasons but she couldn't make a branch grow at a convenient place for her to climb a tree faster than Leo. She had however discovered that she could will a dragon to appear so if she was losing the race she would jump out of the tree and land on the back of a dragon and soar above the clouds. She would send one for Leo and they would soar and dive and explore. This was true happiness. Until....

"Sarah. It's time to get up. You have to have some breakfast. Please darling wake up. We are so worried about you,"

That voice was the inevitable alarm clock, the destroyer of dreams. Saoirse didn't want to be mad at her parents. She knew they loved her and they didn't understand what was going on. Even she didn't know what was going on but she was finally truly happy and they could never understand why.

Chapter Thirteen

"I really am very worried Sarah. You seem to be losing your grip on reality. I warned you this would happen if you stopped your medication. I cannot watch you do any more damage to yourself. Sarah, I'm afraid I'm going to have to discuss with your parents the possibility of you staying in hospital. That way we can ensure you are eating and medicating. There will be someone there at all times if you need to talk." Dr Samnal picked up the phone and requested the presence of Mr and Mrs Hawthorn.

"I don't want to stay in hospital. With all due respect Dr Samnal, I was under the impression that my discussions with you were confidential. I am an adult now and you have no right to confine me to a hospital bed, with or without my parents' permission. I am aware that it is only a dream. I merely expressed a desire that it was real." Saoirse was furious and convinced that everyone was over reacting.

"That isn't quite correct. Your parents are your legal guardians and carers. You have only just turned eighteen and as we cannot be sure of your date of birth it would not take much to persuade a judge of the necessity of your stay. As well as that, you are a danger to yourself and if left untreated you could pose a threat to others. I am sorry but it is for the best and I feel positive that Mr and Mrs Hawthorn will agree. This is for your benefit."

Saoirse protested and yelled and screamed at high volume. This seemed to convince the Hawthorn's of her unstable nature. As Saoirse shrieked, they signed many documents handing over all decision making to the small, ginger haired man with all the answers. Saoirse felt as powerless as an infant, she now understood how wars could be started in the name of power and status. It was a way to protect yourself. She despised being suppressed in this manner and vowed to take control of her life. She tried to storm out of the door but it was blocked by two men, one of whom Saoirse walked straight into. One was holding a straightjacket and the other restrained Saoirse until it was in place and fastened correctly.

"I don't want you to hurt yourself Sarah. The jacket is for your sake, don't fight against it. It will be removed when you have calmed down." That voice! The one that had once been so comforting was now like poison being flicked onto her from the fork of a snake's tongue. She wished she could spit in his face or scratch at his chest until his heart was as pain filled and raw as hers was.

"We are so sorry darling. We just don't know what to do anymore. Don't hate us. You'll thank us some day. I'm sure you will," Mrs Hawthorn was sobbing uncontrollably. She was at a loss at what to do. She did not want her beautiful girl to die or go mad but most of all; she needed her to understand that she had all good intentions.

Saoirse was dragged away as her parent hugged each other and sobbed. They turned to Dr Samnal with pleading eyes full of questions.

"Are you sure this is the only way?"

"I know you love her dearly. This must be so distressing for you but you must understand she is choosing to sleep rather than eat. She is refusing to interact with the real world; she appears to be falling in love with a figment of her imagination. How is she to be truly happy in a world that she refuses to live in. His voice was hypnotic and it comforted the Hawthorne's with an unnatural power.

He suggested that they go home and not visit Saoirse right away, to give her a chance to calm down. They nodded silently and went on their way.

When they were gone Dr Thalious Samnal sat in his swivel chair and sighed. He put his head in his hands and wished that life was less conflicting. As he contemplated his options the image of Dahlia appeared to him as she had taken to do more often.

"I have observed them both together. He doesn't know who she is but if she goes back to him it won't take too long before he figures it out. You must stop her going back. Alessandro is not happy that you have been failing. If Leo finds a way to take her back, Troy will destroy her soul and that will be on your head. Your failure will be her end!"

"Dahlia I am trying everything in my power. I am not as gifted with magic as you and Alessandro. This world has rules. It takes a lot from me to use the magic I do to convince them to turn a blind eye,"

"No excuses! Just stop her going back to Gandros until your King is ready for his sister to return and serve her purpose by his side," At that she left, leaving Thalious hating her just a little bit more. The self-righteous little bog mouse.

In the hospital, they gave Saoirse tablets to prevent her from sleeping. They kept her in a padded room and refused to remove the jacket that strapped her arms around herself and kept her bound tight. There were whispers of suicide watch. They force fed her because she refused to eat and threatened to confine her to a bed with tubes to feed her.

After three days of drug induced wakefulness, Saoirse had a plan of action. She sat calmly in a corner of her white padded room, waiting for the tablet to arrive. When the nurse came Saoirse tried to hide the pills under her tongue. The nurse was wise enough not to fall for it so she was forced to swallow. When she was alone again she concentrated on her throat and stomach muscles and thought of the most revolting smells. Not long later, she was able to regurgitate the chemicals she had unwillingly consumed. She knew she was being watched on camera so she forced herself to work at great haste.

Saoirse sprinted around the room's perimeter as fast as she could, taking small inhales and long exhales, then squeezing her gut; she exhaled all the air in her lungs and ran at the door. Her head hit the only non-padded section of the door, the part that was slid across when people wanted to talk to her or evaluate her. All the actions combined with the collision and lack of breath made Saoirse pass out.

Chapter Fourteen

She succeeded; she was back in Gandros.

"Leo! Leo!" she called out frantically, "Leo where are you?" She needed to know the truth. She had to understand. Most of all she craved with all her existence to know if Leo was real. Was he some figment of her imagination? Could that really be possible? Their bond had grown much stronger since the first meeting. She trusted him more than she trusted herself, but then what if he was herself? She trusted her uncontrollable subconscious to an unhealthy level. Saoirse did not believe she could survive if Leo was not real. It would mean that nothing was real and her only friend was a voice inside her head.

She ran like a lunatic around Gandros. Time could be short. She ran through the fields, in all the buildings and up most of the trees. It was only when she fell to the ground to rub her blistered feet that Leo finally appeared.

Tears fell from her eyes as she bellowed at him for not being there. She demanded to know where he had been along with many other accusations.

"Why can't you be real? Why can't all this be real? Each day I travel from hell to heaven only to find that hell gets much worse each time I go back, I don't want to go back anymore! Why do you make me feel so good only to punish me more severely for enjoying it?" Saoirse was pacing up and down three steps at a time, arms flailing in any direction, her legs were stamping the earth and her lips bullied the air.

Leo approached her and gently placed her arms by her sides, miraculously silencing her at the same time. His eyes stared at her face and waited for her to get caught in his net of calm. Her eyes moved everywhere for a while as though they were replacing her arms, but when she looked at him and saw his bewildered smile she took a deep breath as she had not realised she was so breathless.

"How about we walk and talk, slowly, so that I can understand what the problem is?" He wiped the tears from her cheeks and began to walk with his hand on the small of her back to comfort and guide her.

She explained everything to him. From her lack of sight, non-existent memory and her apparent birth at eight years old in the flames of a burning building. She wept at her guilt of Robbie's legs and her most recent imprisoning to a psychiatric ward.

"So, what you're saying is that you appeared out of nowhere ten years ago with only a necklace as a clue." Saoirse could almost hear his mind ticking. It seemed as though he was piecing together the answer to a very difficult riddle.

"I'm not an idiot. I know I came from somewhere I just don't know where."

Leo was ignoring her, can I see the necklace?"

Saoirse thought it was highly inappropriate that he wanted to admire her jewellery but gave it to him anyway.

He whispered to himself under his breath Saoirse only heard one word or thought she did because it didn't make any sense to her. The word was Ultina.

Leo stared at it as though he could bring the dragon to life and make it speak. When he looked back at Saoirse his expression was odd, almost frightening. There was a brief but strong glimpse of hatred that flashed across his face. When he spoke he was stranger still.

"More things are going on in this world than can be expected by any one, the profits predict some major events though there are small events that gather in time and are allowed to steadily grow. It is they that are the greatest threat to us. They must be found and erased from history so as their course of destruction remains but a thought in some man's head!"

Saoirse had no idea what Leo was speaking of, nor could she understand how a necklace could change someone to such an extent. He knew something. She had a connection with Gandros. Her confusion must have been obvious even through Leo's unfocused eyes. He was staring at the ground so intently he pulled Saoirse's eyes there also, like a needle to a magnet.

Then with an abruptness that startled Saoirse, Leo turned to her and placed his hands tightly on her shoulders squeezing with desperation. When he looked at her he seemed sad and conflicted. Then a resolute expression dominated and he spoke once again.

"I don't know what Gandros is to you. I can't even begin to understand. I don't know if it's an escape, a fantasy, or maybe a joke, but to me it's home. Like the animal I am, I feel bound to protect it in whatever way I can. It is essential that this war is ended or one day I might not have a home to save. What I am about to ask may seem strange, but is essential that you do it, for me.

You will learn things you wish you didn't, you will experience things that you will beg to forget. In doing so however, you may well save Gandros. This is a desperate final plea from a man in need of assistance. Will you come with me to Gandros and help me to find a way to save it from destruction, away from this dream to the real place!"

Maybe it was because he had said come with me, or perhaps it was his begging face, but Saoirse was convinced it was what she must do.

"Leo! I would like nothing better than to stay at Gandros. Tell me how and I will do it." Flashes of her early dreams floated across her mind. Ever since she first set eyes on the beauty of the land she knew she belonged nowhere else.

"I must warn you," Leo began, loosening his grip only slightly, "The times have changed since this memory. You may not like what you see," Leo swallowed his breath as he watched her.

"But at least I will see. I belong here Leo. I know I belong here. I will fight for it!" She threw herself at Leo and gave him a heartfelt hug, "Thank you for making my dreams come true!"

Leo smiled at what she had just said. He finally released her and gave her a suspicious look, "Don't forget I warned you!" Despite his best efforts he could not suppress a grin of gratitude.

"What must I do?" Saoirse asked.

"You must go beyond the edge of reason!"

"I don't understand what you mean!" she said with some apprehension.

"It is very difficult to explain. Close your eyes and let me lead you some where before our time together is extinguished by your other reality."

Saoirse followed with her eyes closed tighter than any palace gates during battle. The next few moments would describe whether or not the risk had been worth taking. There was a breeze that pulled her hair gently backwards as she walked. It was warm and soothing. It gave visions of freedom. After some time, Saoirse peeked through squinted eyes. The view was spectacular.

Leo had led her to Gandros bay. There was a small frame of sand that led to a vast ocean. The tide was high and far and in the distance there were a few magnificent ships. The waves rolled and created a tune that seemed to synchronise with the wind. Parts of the water were warm almost green in colour, while other sections were a passionate blue. Saoirse watched as the white boarder jogged in front of a wave and sank into the sand.

Leo spoke before she had to comment.

"Before I tell you how to get to Gandros, I need you to swear on your life that you will do all that you can for Gandros, even if it means your life. If you do not swear it, I will not take you. But you must understand what you swear."

"I swear on my life to protect Gandros in whatever way I can. I do understand what it means to give my word."

"The way you see things in your dreams is not how Gandros is, but rather how it was. I need you to look into my eyes; this may be a disturbing experience but just trust me, alright?"

Saoirse could think of one reason why that would be disturbing, but was sure it was not the reason he meant. Leo held his hands up for her to grasp. She allowed their fingers to intertwine, their skin touched and unknown by the other, both their hearts beat a little faster. Saoirse unconsciously rubbed her thumb across the side of his hand. She took in the patches of rough and smooth. Suddenly, coming back to reality (in a way) she stopped, but was having trouble looking up at him; she was simply staring at their locked hands.

"Sarah?" he said in a low soothing voice which immediately lifted her gaze.

"Why can't you be real?"

"What makes you think I'm not?"

"I know you're not." Saoirse was thinking back to the conversation with her psychiatrist, "I know that you are something in my head. You are my perfect friend. I mean, how can you be real? I wanted to escape and now you are helping me to do that. I was alone and you came from nowhere."

Leo was silent for a while, "Let me show you just how real I am. I am not as perfect as you seem to think. Now look into my eyes, straight into the pupils. Look nowhere else. It is vitally important!"

Saoirse retightened her grip and stared into the black of his eyes. Everything began to twist, a bit of fear rose in Saoirse but then she remembered she was with Leo, so she was safe. She loved her parents and had grown close to a few people, she had even dated boys when she was feeling more confident but she never truly felt safe except when she met Leo. He now knew everything about her. He knew everything that she knew and he wasn't running away. Instead he wanted her to join him. He knew her strengths and weaknesses, he saw her as a whole person and he wanted her closer to him. She felt happiness seep through the cracks. How had he managed to grow so dear to her she didn't know, but she was willing to allow herself to like it. It was not long before the blackness overpowered all else, temporarily.

When the darkness faded and Saoirse was allowed to look around her again they were in the same place but the difference was extraordinary. The majestic blues were contaminated with orange and red. The playful white was infected with dirty grey. The tide was low and revealed many rocks, bones and skulls, rusting armour, damaged weaponry and a strong smell of obvious defeat on the weaker half.

"What is this?" Saoirse gasped.

"This is the edge of reason. I know it's unnerving but I need to explain to you how to survive."

Saoirse was shocked. It took her a long while to adjust to this raging nightmare compared with the oceanic beauty that had been there only a few minutes before hand.

"At the moment you are in a dream. You are simply a visitor to an art gallery, a mere spectator. If you go through the edge of reason, you cease to exist in the world you know. You cannot travel back; this is your path to Gandros." He waved his arms across the endless trek, "And I do not know for sure if you will be able to see." He did not want to discourage her and the look of disillusionment on her face was killing him.

If I can see now why would I not see when I walk across this, this path?"

"At the moment you are asleep! Don't interrupt. You said you could only see when you were asleep. When you reach Gandros you will be there body and soul. Without the use of magic, no one can survive without sleep for more than a couple of weeks. So, I don't know what will happen when u fall asleep and then wake up again. Now pay close attention. Look around you. Do you see the rocks and the ocean?"

With a hint of impatience Saoirse replied, "I already told you that I could."

"Now, close your eyes. Can you remember the exact position of each of the rocks?"

"Of course I can't!"

"I know you are impatient and I understand that you are afraid. I also know that you want more than anything to have a happy life with memories and sight. I strongly believe that you will get that wish. This is the start of a very long path. Alright now, bend down and feel the rock nearest you."

She felt the rock. The rougher patches and the parts blanketed with sea plants and water animals.

"To get to the real Gandros you must take the smooth path. By that I mean some of the rocks have no plants, no animals and no scars. They are hard to find and will take a lot of energy from you. You MUST feel all of the rock and ignore any sounds that may lead you away. Do you understand?"

"Can I not just follow you?"

"It is not as simple as that."

"Is anything ever simple?"

"This is a glimpse of the edge. You have to wait for it to come to you."

"What do you mean now?" confusion was exhausting her.

Before she had finished her question, the frightening image had dispersed and the picturesque ocean returned.

"You have to do this on your own; I recommend you stay here so that you don't get lost when darkness falls. I have business to attend to so I must leave." He smiled his characteristic grin, took Saoirse's hand and kissed it gently.

"Please Leo. I don't understand," She wept.

"There have been a number of accidental portals created in my world throughout this war. I am guiding you to a way to pass through one of the portals. It will close behind you and bring a bit of balance back to the world. Gandros is the name we give to the land that was conquered by the Slamina bloodline and its main city is called the city of Gandros. It is a real place and I believe that something happened to remove you from this world and I'm bringing you home," He moved closer to her and used his thumb to wipe away her tears, then he extended his hand and cupped her face with his warm and dirty hand. She leaned in to his touch. He touched her forehead with his and she tilted her head closer to him. He whispered to her and his warm breath made her heart race.

"I don't want to lose you Sarah. You have no idea how long I have been searching for you and to find you like this and feel like this. I don't understand why the Gods want to take what remains of my crumbled heart,"

Leo had been searching for the Slamina siblings for so long and to find out that he had been spending time with Saoirse this whole time and not known it he was disgusted with himself, and yet he wasn't sure if he wasn't more ashamed of himself for what he was going to do to this innocent, blind soul. She had no idea what cruelty her family had done. Deep down she was one of them. He knew what he had to do.

"Leo you are crying. I told you I will do this for you. I'm not going anywhere, except to follow you. I....I care for you greatly Leo. I just don't want to fail,"

"Don't lose faith. I'll see you on the other side." Leo smiled his half smile and bowed into oblivion, his eyes were the last to disappear but his touch stayed with Saoirse long after he was gone.

Saoirse sat on the same piece of sand that Leo had left her on for a short time; then she paddled in the shallow edge. After several hours of unbearable boredom, she began to make a sand castle, which turned into a sand estate and then into a sand country. She wasn't sure exactly what she was waiting on. It drove her to despair watching the tide run and return. The sun seemed suspended. It neither rose nor fell. It seemed as though everything was waiting for her to do something, while she in turn was waiting for everything to do something for her.

When her empire was complete, and the roads paved with shells and buildings hollowed out, Saoirse lay back and despite her better judgement she began to think. She thought firstly of Gandros and what she could do, though Leo had not explained what he expected her to do. That train of thought naturally led to Leo himself. Was he real? Why did he have such a reaction to the necklace? From there, her mind took the route of the Hawthorn family, their sacrifices, physical, emotional and financial. The familiar worm of guilt passed through her empty gut once again. To distract herself she mistakenly thought of food. She was unaware of how long it had been since she had eaten but the desire for food was maddening. Her thoughts came back to the guilt. Her stomach rumbled. The thoughts in her head were conflicting and fighting each other and her stomach seemed to have an endless input.

When Saoirse's mind was exhausted from a constant over thinking, something finally happened. The orange from the sun dispersed and infiltrated more of the sky, then the ocean and crept its way onto the sand. Darkness attacked all that the orange and red could not.

The urge to run possessed Saoirse but someone somewhere must have been in the process of empowering the demon of fear because she was rooted to the spot.

Soon everything was empty. Saoirse screamed and was relieved to hear an echo. She was not in empty space. She reassured herself it was just a starless, moonless night. She felt the damp sand and rejoiced in the pleasurable sensation it produced. She let the small grains fall through her fingers. It did not take long for Saoirse to decide to move forward. If she wanted to escape the darkness, she had to travel through it.

Crawling on her hands and knees, Saoirse began her voyage. Her dark, lonely trek on the trail she hoped would lead to answers. It was a slow and tiresome process. There were so many rocks to investigate. Many of them appeared smooth until further investigation proved otherwise. Imperfections were hidden below the surface of the ice cold water.

Any movement was made on all fours. She was too nervous to stand and decided to stay in a position she had most balance and confidence.

There were many sounds. Some like swords clashing, men calling, women screaming and children laughing. It was not very difficult for Saoirse ignore the unfamiliar sounds, though that does not say she was not unnerved by them. She kept her head down and her voice silenced. Her greatest challenge arrived when she had reached the peak of her delirious exhaustion. Her hand repeatedly slipped into the water that had changed from ice cold to almost boiling. Steam engulfed her body and blocked her senses. Her concentration was drifting. Every time she was scalded, she came back to her senses briefly and was tempted to plunge into the water and allow the pain to guide her back to reason and sanity. She had to constantly remind herself why she was torturing herself.

The noise was almost constant and when it stopped Saoirse assumed that it was nearly over. Then a voice came rushing towards her. She knew the voice. It was Leo's. He was telling her she was home and all she needed to do was stand up and walk into the water. She was on the verge of obeying when the thought hit her like a well-aimed arrow, that it was probably a trap. So she re-established her balance and continued touching stones. The voice was persistent and in the end she screamed at it to leave her be. It took an age but eventually, it did.

When Saoirse came across a ledge that was on her path she could suffer the pain no more.

She lay down and gave in to sleep. It was a bizarre thought to sleep within sleep but it was what she needed. She could crawl no further until she had rest.

Chapter Fifteen

She was not sure what to expect. So when Saoirse opened her eyes and saw Gandros just as she left it, she was not sure whether or not to rejoice. Leo had told her it was a war zone. This was as tranquil as she left it. Had he lied, or had she travelled a full circle. Was all that effort for nothing or was she dreaming again? It was hard to decide if she was awake or asleep because technically she was always asleep when she was in Gandros. It was very confusing.

She made the choice to live in the ecstasy of the moment. She was out of the darkness and still had her Gandros. She was sure that Leo would arrive soon and explain things to her. She was right of course. Leo did arrive but not with his air of confidence or his comforting voice. It had the sound of regret and Saoirse was all too familiar with regret.

She walked to his side not sure how to respond to his unusual behaviour. She was cautious and her approach was slow. She touched his upper arm and he turned away.

"I want you to know that my actions were guided by sights I see each day. It seems every minute a new horror story is created. I didn't think that I would have any negative emotions but I do. I hope that the deaths will stop now you have returned. I want you to know my heart was torn in so many ways and I truly believe that I made the right decision. So I am sorry for the way this has to be but I'm not sorry for my choice."

He refused to make eye contact with Saoirse and walked just out of reach, always stepping away from comforting advances and questioning eyes.

"Your real name is Saoirse Slamina. You are sister to the traitor Alessandro and daughter of the deceased king and queen. I asked you to come back and I'm sure you will save lives. You will shortly be taken to prison and your fate will be discussed amongst your captors. Please do not struggle, they have a tendency to use excessive force," he paused before adding "I know I did the right thing."

With those parting words he finally looked at Saoirse, whose arm was suspended mid reach and her mouth was open wide. Her eyes swelled with heartbreak and the familiar feeling of loss was present and strong.

No other words passed between them. Saoirse could not think of what to say. She found this hard to believe and slid to the ground in an emotional paralysis. The wait was short; she heard shouting, marching, and commands and felt herself be shaken to consciousness.

She was so overwhelmed with grief, that she did not have a major reaction to the darkness that also confronted her when she woke. She had finally reached the land of her dreams and she was in a far worse predicament than the one she had left. Trapped in a world she did not understand, blind and being held prisoner, she had the memory of betrayal to ponder on.

She longed for her simple ignorant life on the other side.

Saoirse heard horses and listened as best as she could as she was thrown into an open topped cart. She was bound and gagged but had no will to fight at that time. The trip was unsteady and lengthy. Saoirse sensed that she was not on her own but no-one spoke.

When they stopped Saoirse was the first to be removed from the cart.

"We're going to have fun with you!"

This and other remarks followed Saoirse as she shuffled along beside her prison guards. There was much activity taking place. There were roars of dragons, whining of horses, the sound of shovels, the occasional stifled scream and sound of a leather whip saturated with blood whistling a painful tune.

Saoirse was led down a few steps, pulled to a halt while the man who held her fidgeted with keys and unlocked a squeaky gate. Then they pushed her forward once again. As Saoirse stumbled down the cold heartless stone steps, pictures of pain and suffering hit her with the force of nuclear bomb centred on a small village. She heard the screeches like a dying bird's final squawk, only worse because the screams told of prolonged exposure to unbearable acts of intolerable cruelty. Who were these people? Why do they take such pleasure in the sights, sounds and even smells of such acts of cruelty on a fellow human? For once, Saoirse was glad that she could not see. She was now wishing she could not smell. The scent of death lingered in the air; it surrounded Saoirse as though investigating her worthlessness, scanning her, learning her fears and woes. She heard a voice floating out from a door that lay slightly ajar.

"You may be strong now but when I'm done with you, you will be begging for death. I have an eternity to learn what makes you cry, what makes you scream and just how little effort I have to put in before you tell me what I want to know. Do you want to know the best part? I will enjoy it all and have a smile on my face the entire time. Not sure about you though!" An insane laughter resounded around the room.

Saoirse had been rooted to the spot. She compared herself to a tree in the sense that she was merely a powerless observer. Her captors grinned as Saoirse's face reflected her disgust. Although Saoirse could not see, she knew the sights would be worse than the sounds. The scene was the core of insanity. There was no light other than that used to burn the eyes of soldiers whose eye lids had been cut off in an attempt to find the location of Alessandro. Night was a temporary relief for them. The entire level had a red glow, each turn held host to new methods of torture. People were chained to the floor with water dripping on their pressure points. They were blindfolded and restrained with the strongest steels.

Saoirse was eventually thrown into a tomb of her own. It was saturated in a thick substance that Saoirse quickly and correctly assumed was blood, amongst other things. She landed painfully on her left side and banged her head.

She was unsure how long she was left there, the temperature never changed, the screams never stopped, and manic laughter also seemed endless. She was convinced the wait was another form of cruelty. Her heart rate was erratic; her sightless eyes were constantly darting around her sockets. She could not understand what she had done wrong. No matter how hard she tried she could not figure out why Leo led her there and left her to suffer. Saoirse came to the conclusion that he was real, and neither he nor anyone else in the world was on her side. She was once again alone. It was an entirely different kind of alone.

She drifted off into a restless sleep. In her dream the beaten woman was there and a man. They were on a small wooden row boat. The woman was dressed in a beautiful green dress, to match her eyes, with golden lace trimming. She wore make up that did not fully hide the bruises around her eyes. The man wore a deep blue outfit that made his eyes shine brighter. His dark hair had silver highlights and his rough hand bore a wedding ring different to hers. He held her hand and gently pulled her toward him. They both sat in the middle of the row boat arms around each other while the beautiful woman wept.

"I should have picked you my love. Oh what a mess I have made of things. I was tricked. I was weak."

"Let me make this right. Let me show him pain. Let me ensure that he will never lay a hand on you again. Just say the word and I will protect you. Just say the word my love I beg of you!"

"You have a family to consider, as do I. I have a kingdom to consider."

"They will not think you a weak queen for casting aside the man that beats you. They will stand by you."

"They will not if they hear I am an adulteress, and what of our children. They will suffer, and your wife. She is a good woman. I love you so much but it cannot be. I cherish these moments with you but I fear they may come to an end all too soon." At that the image of the beaten woman turned away from her love and almost seemed to look directly at Saoirse. "I will find my strength," the woman vowed.

Leo was also suffering from the choice he had made. He relied constantly on the reassurance from his oldest friend to convince himself he had done what was right and what was necessary for the good of the peace process.

"Rad she trusted me so completely. She has no idea who she is or what is going on. No one has ever trusted me like she has. How do I go on as though I have done nothing wrong? How can this be right?" He was pacing back and forth, arms moving from his hair to his sides to his mouth biting his non-existent nails.

Rad approached him took his fingers out of his mouth and spoke in a soothing voice, "I trust you completely, more so than her. I have more reason to trust you. She trusted you not because you were you, but because she believed she created you. Once Troy finds the Hoggron Xzenny tribe they will extract her memory and use their power and knowledge to restore the land to the beauty it once was. The way your mother had known and loved it. It will be because of you that your mothers dream will come true. Her family will grow old in a peaceful land. People will see what Troy has done and anyone who has remained loyal to Alessandro this far are sure to convert. You have succeeded Leo. You have started the end of this hell."

"I have enough knowledge of that spell to know that it will consume her soul. She will no longer exist."

"Leo! She came from the other world. Her existence is only a mirage. She died many years ago. Now rest yourself. Troy wishes to speak with you first thing tomorrow."

Her voice was always rational. Her logic was almost always flawless. She had a power over Leo ever since they first met in that stone room all those years ago. This time, however he could not settle.

"I cannot retire now. I need to walk, alone. My thoughts are scattered and I need to organise them. I will speak with you tomorrow. Thank you again for your wise words."

As Leo walked the empty streets he wondered if Saoirse was in the same cell in which he had been imprisoned. He could understand what thoughts would be going through her head. As he thought about Saoirse he began to beat his cranium with his fists.

"Get a hold of yourself. You did the right thing. It should have happened sooner. You should have understood long before she handed you the necklace."

Usually, when Leo talked aloud to himself he could convince himself of almost anything. That was why he believed that bringing many of Alessandro's soldiers to their death was the right thing to do. This time he could do nothing but think of her. What would be happening to her at this very moment? He needed to explain the situation to her. Troy would not be very happy. He was under strict orders to stay away from her mind. His only job was to find Alessandro and those who remained loyal to him.

Leo walked for many miles without acknowledging his path. He knew the land well and had lived comfortably in Troy's protection. In return for food, bed and board for himself and Rad, his job was to search and be silently obedient. He learnt early on not to ask questions because although answers were offered he usually didn't like them.

Troy's base was in a mountainous area, with a forest nearby for hunting and wood supply. It was at enough of a distance not to hide any defensive threats. You could see the ocean from the top of the main building but again, it was a trek for any advancing army and they would be seen long before they were in range. It was a great defensive fort.

Leo took refuge beneath a standing stone and concentrated on Saoirse. It had been a week since he had contacted her and was afraid to face her rejection. He would just watch, not make himself known. Maybe speak from a distance, to get his explanation out.

He had to wait a long time. The moon was high and the light surrounded Leo. He always thought the moon looked irritated at being forced to reflect the suns light. The stars were sparse but represented many ancient prophecies. Leo wished he could translate them and make a simple path in life for himself but alas, that was a job for astrologers; if there were any left. They probably knew what was coming and found a place to hide until the storm had passed.

Saoirse's dream was set during dusk, the shadows were long and every colour had dulled as though they did not have a vaccine against the misery. Leo found Saoirse at the lake where they had first met. She was so still; so pathetic. Her tears mixed with the rain that had started to lash down like whips punishing Saoirse for her trusting nature. The lake water rose a little and the ripples that the rain made seemed violent as though they wanted to transform into a tsunami and just needed a fraction more negativity to morph into one. The sight made Leo think of his mothers' final dream, how she had just kept walking into Alessandro's mouth. How his words had caused her death. Were his actions any better? Or were they worse?

"Why are you here?" Saoirse made no sign that she intended to move and spoke so quietly that Leo barely heard her.

"I don't know." He also remained still.

"You have a unique smell. I always know when you're nearby."

"It's called self-loathing."

"It's not just yourself that loathes you."

Leo didn't know what to do. Should he go over to her? Should he apologise. Would she believe his sincerity?

"Saoirse I really am sorry."

"Sorry?" She almost laughed. She turned and stood tall, "You dare to tell me that you're SORRY. You led me to torture. You showed me the path to a deeper level of hell; the part of hell that I can't wake up from. I used to cry, because I thought you didn't exist. I hate you. I truly hate you. I pray each night for the power to kill you with my bare hands!"

She was furious, her fists were clenching and releasing. Her eyes were as red as her boiling blood.

"Leave my dream. Leave my thoughts and for God's sake leave... Just leave!"

He stood resolute. "I know where you are. I'm going to come and rescue you. I give you my word."

"Your word has no worth in my world."

"I swear it."

"I'll kill you."

"I'll prove myself to you. Earn your forgiveness."

"Leave Now!"

As he left, Saoirse crumbled into a heap; emotionally and physically destroyed.

"Why?" she whispered again and again, "Why?"

Leo had made up his mind. He left her but vowed to return. He had no plan but knew someone that would help him. He was going to save her. No matter what the consequences!

Chapter Sixteen

Thalious got the call that Sarah Hawthorn had had an accident in the padded room. He started to panic. How was it even possible to put yourself into a coma in a room covered in padding? This was bad very bad. It had been hard enough to convince his colleagues to keep Sarah in a drug educed wakeful state. It had taken a lot of magic to manipulate their minds, almost as much as was needed to convince a lot of people that he was a qualified psychiatrist. He had followed Sarah to the hospital all those years ago and got the idea whilst eves dropping on a conversation between her doctors.

Sarah had lapsed into a coma and her parents wanted to vent at him and demand answers. How could he explain to them that it wasn't actually his fault and that Sarah, as he had grown accustomed to calling her, had fallen asleep and gone to another world, her world, the one she was cast out of over ten years ago, forbidden to return until the time was right. Alessandro was not going to be happy. He was sure to know. As he was thinking these thoughts, an apparition of a young woman appeared before him.

"Dahlia! I assume you already know that she has returned?" Thalious bowed his head in shame.

"You have failed us. It is not safe for her to return at this time. We now have to find her and secure her until she is of use to us."

"I am ashamed. I tried my best alas my best is far from good enough."

"We agree. That is why we have decided your punishment is to remain here. Never to return to Gandros as you may have destroyed any chance of returning it to its glorious state with the rightful king on the throne."

"No, No I can fix this. I can make it right. Give me a chance to wake her up from here." This was not his world, he had carried out his duty without complaint or flaw for so long, how could they treat him this way? All he wanted was to return home and reap the rewards of his hard work. He had not participated in a proper duel in so long. This world fought differently, he did not understand their rules. Nature was hidden in manmade patches and mighty beasts were tamed as pets. He missed the sights of dragons and bloodshed and he strongly desired to use his axe once more.

"We have altered our plans. We need you to kill her here so she will be trapped in Gandros. We can't risk her returning to this world and then refusing to come home when we need her. Do your duty well one last time and we may change your sentence."

At that, the image of Daliah evaporated and left Thalious with a choice, to kill the girl he had watched grow up, the girl he had guided and protected and dare he say it even grown to love. He watched with admiration as she grew into a strong woman and stood tall in the face of all adversities. If he didn't, there was no chance of his returning to his homeland. With a heartfelt sigh he walked out of his office and made his way to Sarah's bedside to speak to her parents and lie to them that everything was going to be alright.

Chapter Seventeen

Saoirse was feeling emotions she had always felt though on a much deeper level. She did not know how long she had been imprisoned, it could have been weeks or months or maybe even just days. She had flashbacks that forced her to relive the same agony repeatedly she did could not fathom whether it happened as often as she felt or if it was all in her mind. Her dreams sometimes allowed her some comfort, but even they betrayed her. Saoirse's body had endured unbelievable methods of pain. Some were psychological, most were physical. She had no nails on her fingers or toes and screamed as she vividly remembered the feeling of the thin flesh being torn. She was already blind so escaped some forms of torture. She wept constantly, just as she had as a child in the hospital. Why would she want to remember a life that could bear any resemblance to this hell?

She was woken once more by a wart scared hand and a strong smell of animal faeces. Her arm was pulled from its socket soothed only by her long loud screech, luckily though it popped back into place not long after it had left.

"There is some one here to collect you! I'm sorry we didn't get to see more of each other," he sneered.

Saoirse felt sick at his tone of voice and wished she could slap him across his dirty face; to close his drooling mouth; to blacken his filthy eyes and turn his foul body into an uglier corpse. She worried about what was to become of her. She had listened to guards talk about Troy. They held him in such high esteem. What had he done to deserve the allegiance of so many?

She had so far learnt that Alessandro was her brother and he was the blood heir to the throne and Troy had challenged his ability and motives. Alessandro was on the run, but still proving to be a great threat.

"Just you wait until Troy gets a hold a ye. Ye'll soon r'member den. Ne more a this other world nonsense."

He pulled Saoirse along at a speed she was sure was not necessary. He kept slowing then suddenly rushing; which made Saoirse trip and slip. Her shoulder was still stinging. She managed to survive the steep flight of steps and waited without saying a word as her captor unlocked the iron gates. The hinges groaned loudly.

"Well ere she is. Full a nonsense completely mad. Don see how she'll be o much use." Saoirse felt pride in her lack of assistance, even if it did result in much agony.

"There are a lot of things that you don't see Krag. Now if you don't mind, I have a long way to go."

That voice! That pompous, overconfident tone. Saoirse recognised him immediately. Her anger gave birth to a dirty blood infected spit where she thought Leo was standing.

The man now identified as Krag hit Saoirse across the face with the back of his hand. He barely had time to live in the joy of the moment when Leo punched him square in the nose.

"She is in my charge now. You have no right to punish without my say!"

"Ye may 'ave escaped me all those years ago but yer not better than me. Ye are jus an errand boy. I do the real business."

"Apparently, not very well. Have you figured out how I got away yet? No! I am better than you! Now get me a horse for the prisoner!"

"How do ye expect a blind girl to ride?"

"Do you expect me to walk? Now go or shall I tell Troy you were not very co - operative?"

With reluctance, he left. As the sound of his steps lowered Saoirse made an attempt to talk but Leo was quicker than her.

"Not a word. Not yet."

As Leo looked at Saoirse he was amazed at how she could still have such fight in her after what she had endured. He still felt awful that he had been the one to put her here, but if only she knew what he had been through so far to try to right the wrong.

After he had visited her dream, he had sprinted back to Troy's fortress and went straight to the house that Rad had recently moved into. It was large with a small private plot of land, a gift from Troy. It had been built along with others like it, to make people feel more settled. It gave an image of security and permanent prosperity. He gave no thought to the late hour and began his desperate attack on Rad's door. Her dog started to howl and scrape at the bottom of the door. Leo saw its snout sniffing the gap beneath the door.

Eventually, a glow from a candle had approached the window. Rad opened the door and was quite obviously not impressed. Her hair was flung haphazardly in various directions; she had dark patches under her eyes. Early rising seemed to make her age. The flickering candle emphasised her snarl.

"What could possibly be wrong at this time?"

"I need your help."

"And I need sleep. We don't always get what we need!"

"Please Rad. I have to rescue her. There has to be a way to end this without her getting hurt. There just has to be. Help me find it. Please."

"Leo it is late, sleep now, think of everything you want to give up, we can talk tomorrow after you talk to Troy." Leo made to debate, but was stifled, " I am no use to you now, please sleep on it, speak with Troy and we will discuss your woes at a decent hour," she stressed the "decent hour." "You can sleep here, now go on, sleep."

She kicked the dog that had been constantly barking since Leo's arrival as she made her way back to bed. Leo missed the pup he had rescued all those years ago. He thought he was doing the right thing by giving it a chance at life; it grew to be a big strong dog and was devoted to Leo, stupidly devoted to Leo; Just as Saoirse had been. Not long after Leo and Rad had finally found Troy Leo had gone hunting. He was looking for deer but what he found was a large, angry bear determined to protect her young. It had charged at him swiping its giant paws and sharp claws. His faithful dog had lunged at it and chased it away while Leo escaped. He spent months searching for the dog but he never found her.

Leo lay down to rest, though sleep evaded him. He tossed and turned on the floor and got up to pace but became nervous of bothering Rad. In the end, he lay awake listening to the sounds of the night. There were insects chippering, owls hooting, mice scuttling and Rad snoring. How does anyone sleep with all this activity?

When the sun rose, Leo went to the main hall, Troy was already having breakfast with some of his fighting men, Troy had a table to himself on a raised platform placed horizontal to the tables below, that were lined with many strong men. The floor was lined with straw and the dogs gnawed on leftover food. A few rats ventured from the outskirts to try and retrieve food. Most met the disastrous digestive system of the hungry hounds.

"Ah Leo. Good. Good. Join me for a meal. I have an announcement to make and I am glad you have arrived in time to hear it."

Leo sat but did not eat. His thoughts were in hyper drive. He knew he couldn't get Saoirse out the way Rad and himself had escaped over a decade ago. There just wasn't enough time. If Troy knew what he was doing he would lose all the protection that he provided. He also had a lot of enemies that far exceeded his skill in hunting and hiding.

"As you all know for many years now, I have been searching for the whereabouts of the original Hoggron Xzenny tribe," Troy began, "They have knowledge and skill that I did not have time to learn before my mentors were so maliciously murdered. However, I now know that their base is hidden somewhere in the Shay Lou forest. It is a large area; so I am sending small search parties to inconspicuously look for an entrance. As well as that glorious news, I am sure you have heard the rumours that Saoirse Slamina is in my custody. Those whispers are correct. She was found by our very own Leo Dovinpoir. We congratulate him for this; however, he was given strict instructions to stay away from her after the capture." He looked Leo straight in the eye and watch the realisation gradually cross his face, "He failed to obey."

All eyes were now on Leo. He jumped to his feet and quickly evaluated his chances of escape or manipulation.

"I want you all to look upon him now and see him as a traitor."

The two men closest to Leo grabbed him and twisted his limbs in a successful attempt to restrain him.

"I have given him much and he has until now been a loyal aid. Now though, he is a liability. He has the desire to destroy our only hope of quickly returning our beloved land back to its beauty and prosperity. The way we all long for it to be, for ourselves and our families. We have Saoirse. We nearly have the Hoggron Xzenny chiefs. We are near the end to all our suffering. All we have longed for; he wishes to destroy. Without Saoirse, we may well starve before we can plant enough food to feed everyone."

There were shouts of displeasure; angry calls for his head and threatening movements and gestures.

"Throw him to the pits and let him starve to death."

There was a loud cheer as Leo was lifted off his feet. He was screaming for an explanation or a chance to explain.

"There has to be another way! There is another way. She doesn't deserve this!"

His pleas fell on deaf ears. The men were so stained by war they were addicted to blood and punishment. He passed Rad at the door. She seemed confused to see him in such a state.

"You betrayed me? You send me to my death just as I try to right my wrong! You do this to me! I curse you and all who dare to care for you!" Leo's rage was obvious and its poisonous spit stung Rad.

"Leo I did no such thing."

He was dragged out of vocal range but his words were not hard to imagine as Rad knew him well.

The pits were at the far west of the dungeons. It was not a cell. It was much worse. It was at a lower level and the ground was not paved. The soil was constantly damp. There was no escape from it. Part of what made the experience so terrible was that the only door in or out was ten foot above the head of the average male. Prisoners were pushed in and usually broke a bone or two when they landed. There was no light and no holes to ventilate the area and worst of all no prospect of food. The only moisture was what was in the soil. There must be a river somewhere close by as it was constantly moist. Not even the rats chose to enter this level. The conditions were perfect for decomposing corpses; which never left their unceremonious grave. The smell was intolerable.

Leo prepared himself for the fall and landed with minimal damage. Nothing was broken but his wrist was sprained. He had wished a curse upon every one he passed. He claimed he would haunt their dreams and send them insane with his nightly visits. They all laughed at him and placed bets about how long he would last and who would get his possessions. One of the many degrading aspects of being sent to the pits was that you were stripped. In harsh times clothing was a luxury.

When Leo had finished cursing everyone else he began to curse himself for not having any allies. All his work had been to gain strength for Troy, but not once did he think of protection for himself in the event that Troy turned against him. He had always viewed himself as an irreplaceable part of Troy's army. He could fight (So could most men that had survived this far). He could ride (again not unique), but he was the only one who could hunt true traitors. Now he was one. How can Troy think of getting the most from a search party or a raid or torture without him? Part of his job was to prevent prisoners from resting when they passed out.

For the entire day, there was no noise. Leo had no clue as to whom, if anyone was guarding him. He did not sleep. He did not lie down. His feet were growing numb. His hatred gave him strength, but no mental direction. When he heard voices his ears automatically tuned in. If he recognised them they would be the first to experience his haunting.

"Why don't you take this and go for a long toilet break?"

"I cannot accept a bribe to set him free."

"It's not to set him free. I just want a little visit. A woman needs to say goodbye to her special friend; If you catch my meaning."

There was a pause as the guard weighed his options and duty against the size of the bag handed to him. Leo held his breath during these tense few seconds. It was worse than watching a snail crawl. Time he discovered was a deceitful tease, the world's greatest actor.

"I'll have to lock you in. I can't leave the door unlocked and unattended."

"And what if you don't let me out?" Leo could almost see the pouting look she was giving the guard.

"You'll have to take that risk."

"Don't you trust me?" He was sure she would be stroking his arm by now.

"No."

"I'm keeping the ladder in place." She hated not getting her way.

The turning of the key made Leo's heart stop and his breath slow, giving the impression of the waking dead. The rusty hinges threw sparks in the air. A gust of refreshing wind blew around the confined space adding an eerie chill to Leo's damp body.

Rad appeared in the shallow torch light and threw down a ladder made of plaited rope and ingenious knots. The door slammed closed as soon as her body was through the frame. She landed lightly; Glad of her shoes.

"Well this is a familiar sight," she was nervous and Leo said nothing to calm her. He was still in a state of deathly shock. "I had nothing to do with this Leo. I swear to you. I never revealed your intentions to Troy nor anyone else for that matter!"

"Then how did he know?"

"Perhaps it was extracted from Saoirse?"

"How would word reach him so fast?"

"Some riders have great skill."

"She was still asleep when I left her."

"That means nothing."

"I can think of a way that makes the pieces fit." He gave her a knowing glance.

"It is highly doubtful that he created a path into people's dreams. You know yourself it is a rare gift.

"A gift that was given by magic."

"A level of magic that has not been seen in many years. Far beyond Troy's reach."

"Over a decade of research is bound to provide some results."

"I cannot deny there is some logic to it. I came here for a reason other than debate. Do you still wish to go to her aid?"

"I do; but I don't see how."

"A rider had been sent to escort Saoirse here. Once in custody there will be a spell to bind them together until she arrives here and Troy agrees to the detachment. If you are quick, you can overtake him. Arrive there first. Here is a duplicate of the letter written by Troy. Do not create a scene. You must claim to be there on Troy's behalf. Leave at a walk until you are out of sight then gallop with as much haste as you can muster. I have no idea what you can do after that. You will have made enemies on all sides. That is why I insist that you take Flaragin. She has a great bloodline and unbelievable endurance over tough terrain. She is well trained and will serve you well."

"Why do you still insist on saving me and guiding me?"

"I tried for so many years to escape. It was only with your help that I escaped and could build a great life. I am envied by many; and I like it." She smiled.

"You risk it all now!"

"Put your mind at ease. Let us talk of good times until the guard returns."

They talked of anything but ill omens. They reminisced but did not say good bye. Neither had the heart to say what they were genuinely thinking. It was another flaw in man's genetic makeup.

"If you want out at all it had better be now." The guard had returned and seemed disappointed that he had not interrupted anything.

"The time has passed too quickly for my liking,"

Rad began as she climbed the ladder, "For now I must do what my heart and head say is wrong."

"He went against Troy's ruling. Have no sympathy for the boy."

"It is not for the boy that my conscience is torn." The guard made an attempt to reach for his sword but alas, it was too late. "With all that I am, I am sorry." she said this as the sharper end of the double-bladed dagger cut through his intestines and up towards his lungs. His out of shape physique made the cut smoother as there was more fat than muscle.

As he stared down at his wound he saw the true colour of his own blood. His intestines fell to the ground before his strength left his legs. With as much discomfort for the observer as nails on a black board his knees fell heavily on top of his organs. Leo, who had climbed the ladder, cringed as the blood splashed into his eyes and onto his tongue. He vomited on top of the mess before him.

"I am sorry," he managed to whisper as the life left the victim's body. The sense of hearing is said to be the last to go, if that is true then the guard carried with him a whole hearted apology and a deep rooted hatred.

"Flaragin is in her usual stall. I have her saddled already. All I ask of you is one favour." The two friends were walking fast along the edge of the halls. Leo had found some suitably fitting clothes and was trying to hide behind Rad.

"Name it Rad. Please. It would be my honour."

"Swear to do it; No matter what."

"I swear upon my freedom."

"Do not tell Saoirse of the outcome of the spell. You will take her from Troy so please do not reveal what was to be her fate."

"I cannot in good conscience conceal that from her!" Leo was outraged at being asked to do something so immoral, especially now that he was trying to be a better person.

"You have already sworn it., upon your freedom. Choose now, conceal it or concede your fate!"

They were but a few feet away from the stable that held Leo's only escape.

"I am grateful for all you have done for me. Though you must know I will not forgive you for the conditions you place upon my freedom. You know I can do nothing to help her from the pits."

"Just go."

Leo had barely taken two steps when she called him back. He stood where he was watching the deserted area. She ran to him. Lifting her right arm and gently brushing his cheek as she placed it behind his neck. Her left arm lay suspended half way between his waist and his neck. She brushed her lips against his, her eyes were closed.

Leo had not expected this. It was not his first kiss but he did not move. He made no attempt at first but then his lips joined hers in their romantic movements. He could not organise his emotions. He had never thought of Rad in that way, and there was no point now because they were heading on to two different paths. He wrapped his arms around her and pulled her closer. Suddenly he wanted time to stand still so this moment could last just a little longer. He made to move away but she pulled him toward her and then pushed him against the wall and kissed him with so much passion it would have been impossible for any man not to get caught up in the moment. She pushed her hips against him, then with no warning, rested her head below his chin and placed her hands on his shoulders and without opening her eyes Rad told him to go.

"Do not forget me but do not dwell. Our chapter has ended. Take care of Flare. I broke her in myself."

Leo had mounted the horse without knowing what to say, he sat tall with his back straight and legs long. The mare was dancing on the spot and Rad was forced to slap the horse's hind quarters to make her move into an energetic trot. The horse lifted her front legs high and had a regular rhythm to its pace. Leo looked back only once. The clothes he was wearing were crawling with lice and made his skin itch like mad.

Chapter Eighteen

He left the main buildings behind him. Then the small market stalls and finally the smaller dwellings on the dangerous outskirts. At first, he concentrated on manoeuvring his mount onto the softer ground to muffle the sound of her steps. After a while, he realised her hoof prints might be followed so when he was far enough out he galloped in zig zag patterns, through puddles, round trees over rocks and then followed the tracks of other animals. If he was going to be followed, it wasn't going to be easy. When he was convinced he would confuse even Rad herself he concentrated on covering as much ground as possible. He headed towards the mountain at high speed.

After Leo was out of sight Rad turned to Troy and said, "It is done. He will succeed where we have failed. He will find Alessandro and lead us to him."

"And how do you feel betraying a boy you care for?" Troy asked with a jealous expression on his face.

"Oh Troy, you were not well hidden I could not have him see you. It would," she paused as she stepped close to him, "Complicated things."

Troy was taller than her and when he looked down at her and saw breathing deeply he could not help himself. He picked her up as he had done many times before kissing her lips and her neck and took her to the now vacant stable without any thought about who was manipulating whom.

After a while, Leo slowed to a walk. Flaragin tried to nibble at the bushes as they passed by. When they came to a river Leo rode up for a mile and then back down to ensure that there were no dead animals contaminating the water and then he and Flare took a drink. While his horse drank deeply, Leo tried to clean up his attire. The clothes were loose on him but at least they didn't make it too obvious that he was an escaped prisoner. Not that there was a stereotypical view of what people in that situation should look like. He checked that he still had the letter safely stored in a pocket, folded and with the wax seal still intact. Leo was mildly curious as to how Rad had come by the seal. She must have risked a lot for him. Why though had she chosen to kiss him when they were probably never going to meet again? Maybe that was why. It was a passionate farewell.

He looked over at Flaragin. Even her reflection glowed with health. The movement of her throat muscles made her coat shimmer as she drank. A few leaves fell from the overhanging branches. One landed on her unsaddled back. She shivered and it floated down to her two tone hooves. They were mostly white with vertical black lines of varying width. Leo walked over to her crushing the daisy stained grass as he went. He patted her neck to let her know the rest was over. She lifted her head and snorted into the cool air. Leo saddled her up and she stood with no complaints.

A day had gone by before Leo caught up with the original messenger. He had taken a lower path. Leo rode quietly as he walked along the edge of a narrow path. He prayed that no pebbles would fall. The man looked as though he was in desperate need of a rest. His animal was hyper. Hard to control and covered in thick white sweat. Before long, he dismounted and tied the chestnuts reins around a bare bush. He filled his water container from a nearby stream and sat a safe distance from his ride which was stamping his feet and shaking his head more vigorously now that he had been tied. He put his head down and drifted into an exhausted sleep.

Leo took a path down to the sleeping man. Dismounted and untied the stallion. He was difficult to handle but as soon as they were hearing distance away, Leo let the stallion go. With a smile of satisfaction, Leo set off again confident he would reach his destination before long and certainly before the messenger could raise the alarm.

As the sun stretched itself out across the edge of the world and allowed darkness to supervise its kingdom. Leo lay down to rest. He thought of Saoirse and before long he was in her dreams again. He thought he should prepare her for his arrival.

He stayed at a distance and watched as she pulled petals from flowers. He heard her say, "Traitor," and pull a petal then. "Saviour," and pull another one. When the flower stood naked before the world she threw away the shameful stem and with the ball of her foot ground it into the dirt saying, "Traitor! Traitor!"

He absorbed her misery just as she absorbed the lashing rain she had created. The lake made angry faces as it was repeatedly pounded. The entire atmosphere was grim. She was so beyond herself she could not even sense Leo's presence.

It is sad to witness how fast betrayal and depression can attack at a vulnerable personality. Saoirse, much like Gandros had been reduced to a mere outer shell in a very short space of time. Leo's guilt pulled harder at his heart strings and took control of a larger percentage of his thoughts. He woke himself up and forced himself to endure more of the journey. She really had cared for him. How could he have done this to her? Why did he do it? It was true that there would soon be a worldwide shortage of food but some people were so glutinous he hated them. Surely they could put something in place now before it really was too late. Troy could call off his dragon searches. They were a big reason for crop failure. It's hard for crops to survive fire. Alessandro could stop poisoning Troy's water supply and food rations. Wasn't that something a true leader should do? Shouldn't a leader put his people first? Neither Alessandro nor Troy had thought about the long term effects of this war and each of them seemed more preoccupied with killing the other and winning a title than protecting the land. Sure Troy had built some houses but they are only for those he deemed worthy.

These thoughts and many more kept Leo awake as he tried to remember the way to his childhood hell. He came across the Tingh River. When he and Rad had crossed it all those years ago there had been a bridge, part of a bridge. It had been made of stone and wood with columns going direct from the bottom of the bridge into the raging river. The frame of the bridge had remained but the planks of wood that had been used to walk on had been burnt to ash. It was at this point that Leo had learned Rad could not swim. She was petrified of the water. He had thought she was not afraid of anything the bravest person he knew. She was confident she could find Troy and always seemed to have the answers. She was the one who had helped him to nurture his gift. She was the one who gave him belief in himself. Without her he most likely would not have been able to find Troy's followers dreams and in turn find Troy. Without Leo, Troy would not have the stronghold he has now. He just had to remember that people change, times change, loyalties change, except Rad. She was forever loyal to him.

He was so grateful to her. She helped him even though she had those secret feelings for him. She was risking a lot for him. He would find a way to make it up to her.

It had been a nerve racking experience walking along the unstable stone work of the bridge. Leo came up with the idea to tie something around themselves so if one fell they both fell. That way they would not be separated.

"Leo, I don't want us both to die," Rad had responded to his suggestion.

"Rad, I can't find my way without you. If you fall, I fall with you. So don't fall," he had laughed.

"How can you be so chipper when we are going to die in a horrid watery grave?" She was both irritated and impressed by his optimistic outlook.

"Rad. How can you doubt that the Gods are on our side? We escaped that awful place. We found out where Troy's stronghold is. We are on our way to find him. He will welcome us as though we were guardians of the realm. We will be treated like his kin; and best of all Rad I have seen Alessandro. I have a fresh connection to him. It will not be long before I can end him. So if you think that I will let this flowing puddle get in the way of my revenge you are mistaken. Trust me my friend. We will survive and we will destroy Alessandro Slamina,"

After much debating they had made the difficult choice to walk back to the city of Gandros and steal some rope and if they were lucky a couple of planks of wood. In the end they had not needed to walk all the way back as they robbed a building full of supplies on the way. They had wrapped the rope around themselves and started across the large river some sections were so badly damaged they had had to jump. There were numerous times each of them had thankful for the rope; when they had got across the river Rad had collapsed in a heap.

"You are as mad as a woman bitten by scorn,"

"But we are alive are we not?" Leo had fallen into a fit of manic laughter. He had been scared out of his wits but it had paid off.

That had been how they got across before and Leo heard the echo of his childhood laughter. It was not how he could get across now. There was barely a cart load of rubble above the water to mark what had been a glorious bridge. It had brought much business to Gandros City and helped many people to prosper before the downfall.

He dismounted and ate some of the supplies Rad had provided for him while Flare munched on the shoots of grass that had started to grow through the ash. There had to be some way to get across. There was no way that the land had been permanently segregated. The air was cold and the river raced at such a speed that it spat a fine spay over those near it. It was both refreshing and painful. Leo wondered if this had once been a place that families came to picnic during the time of peace. He could almost see the ghosts of past enjoyment float across his vision; he could almost see children and couples in love on boats enjoying the current of the river. One was so clear he could hear the voices of men swearing and oars splashing.

It took him a while to come out of his pensive reminiscing to see that there really was someone in a boat crossing the river. They had goats and sheep in the boat with them and were fighting against the water and the rain that had started to pour. "Perfect." Leo thought. He watched their progress and met them when they arrived at his side of the water.

"Do you make this journey often?" Leo tried to sound approachable and cheerful.

"What's it to you?" the two men asked suspiciously in unison.

"I was just thinking that if you got a large rope and tied it to the tree at one end and the tree at the other then you could pull yourself along using the rope as a guide. It would save you a lot of time and hassle."

The two men looked at each other but didn't speak.

"There was once a rope works on the way to the city of Gandros that had been abandoned. Perhaps there is still rope there not yet salvaged that you could tie together and use."

Again the men looked at each other and then back to Leo with the same quizzical expression.

Leo sighed and rolled his eyes, "If you take me and my horse across the river I will show you where it was."

The men must be telepathic Leo thought because they looked at each other and spoke in unison, "Alright then,"

Leo waited impatiently while they unloaded their animals and gave hand signals to their collie dog that the dog seemed to understand. The dog rounded up the animals and kept them together standing in the shape of a heart. Leo thought that although it was impressive it was quite odd that they taught the dog to round them up in such a way.

They got across the river with an unsteady Flare and Leo led them to the abandoned rope work house. If they were lucky it would not have been completely looted. It was out of the way and hidden by a lot of destruction, so it was possible. He left them at the entrance and in together once more they spoke, "Thank you, boy,"

'boy' pah he was more of a man now than a boy surely! As they walked away Leo wondered if they were brothers and that's why they could read each other's minds but as they disappeared the slightly taller of the two took the other by the hand and they linked their fingers and laughed while smiling to one another. Leo felt sure they had made some kind of a joke about him but couldn't figure out what it was. Perhaps they could read his mind and were laughing at the idea that he thought they were brothers.

He continued on his journey, passing through what remained of the great city. It really was so different to Saoirse's dreams. There were fewer corpses than when he had travelled through a decade ago but then there was less of everything; less beauty, less hope, less buildings, less life. He kept pushing forward until he reached Saoirse's prison, his prison, where he had sent her.

Chapter Nineteen

Saoirse was furious, how could he have sent her here if he had been here himself? If he knew what it was like? If he had experienced it himself what could make him send her to the same fate? Why had he come back for her? Was it another trick? Or was it genuine concern?

The sound of metal on stone came before long. The horse's steps chipped away at the stone it walked on. There were two voices not one. What was going to happen now?

"Who is this? Do you need protection?" Saoirse missed the look of murderous loathing that Leo received.

"This's Erik. He gonna perform de bindin spell. Tha means if she dies ye die. Ye better hope she don hav ne accidents."

Saoirse sensed that Leo had either not planned on this or had hoped to avoid it. The new horse reared up, revealing his muddy stomach, overgrown hooves and baring its uneven teeth. It was pulling away from Krag and the leather bridle strained to hold the pressure. Saoirse was emotionally numb now and physically sick. Leo was furious.

"Is that the safest mount you have? Has it even been broken?"

"It's tha only one on offar to ye. Take it or walk!"

Leo walked over and patted the dun on the neck. He went to the girth and unbuckled it and removed the saddle. He put gentle pressure along the equines back. The horse was not happy. His spine dipped at the slightest touch. He turned his head and bit Leo hard on his thigh.

"This horse is broken alright! What did you do to it? Fall from the mountain? This horse is only good for meat. Not that there's much of that either!"

"Tis the only one on offer."

"I'll take it if only to prove your worthlessness to Troy!"

So it was true Saoirse thought. He had come on Troy's behalf.

Without any warning Saoirse felt her feet lift from the ground. She felt pressure around her waist, a firm grip. As she was suspended in the air she began to scream and kick. Her foot made contact with Flaragins hind quarters and made her step forward noisily.

"Stop screaming and lift your leg as high as you can." Leo scolded then added in a softer tone, "It's alright Sarah."

Why did mentioning a familiar name calm her a fraction? When Saoirse's legs were on either side of the horse she felt hysterically for the mane and wrapped her arms around the thick neck. She spread her weight across the horse's front and tensed all her muscles. It wasn't long before Leo was up behind her. He had tied the reins of the spare horse to his stirrup leather and wrapped his arms around Saoirse pulling her into a sitting position. Her back was pressed up against his chest; her head was to the side of his, her hands were now on the pommel of the saddle. She felt his warm breath pass her face. She felt his confident breathing trying to hide his rapid frightened heart rate. He turned his head and hovered by her cheek before moving gently to her ear he whispered, "Hold on tight and be prepared." The air from his nose went down her neck, his grip tightened around her stomach.

"Now that the two of you are touching it will take a few minutes to bind you." His voice was old but he moved swiftly, "I need to tie your wrists together."

Leo lent forward slightly and squeezed his horse straight into a gallop. Unprepared and supported only by Leo and her grip on the saddle Saoirse kept slipping from one side to the next. Leo kept correcting her position. She was bouncing all around and her fragile body gave out warnings to her head that it could not take much more abuse. The hands of their enemies kept reaching out trying to grab at the horse, but they were moving too fast for anyone to stop them.

When they were heading up a steep hill, Leo told her to lean as far forward as she felt comfortable. They moved so quickly they did not hear Erik turn to Krag and say, "Troy was right. How long do we wait?"

"Give 'im a good 'ead start. He has a lot o' work ta do." They laughed as they watched the decreasing size of Leo and Saoirse.

When Leo reached the top of the third rise, he slowed to a good paced walk, "I need you to sit very still, we are passing a dangerous path and I need to let the horse find her own footing and the light is beginning to fade. Just be still and think good thoughts."

Leo did not elaborate further. He did not mention that they would soon be on a steep incline up the side of a very vertical drop with barely enough room for one horse let alone two. To the right, waves crashed at least fifteen foot up towards them. Rocks were sharp and could easily cut through human flesh. The wind sang a rough tune and battered them into the side of the cliff face. It was only a few hours passed midday, but the light was fading fast. Bats screeched their gothic call. The horses miraculously stayed unspoken. On a few occasions, Flaragin stumbled and made Saoirse scream through fear sown lips.

They trekked along this terrifying trail for a tedious length of time. Saoirse was ready to drop off to sleep. She felt so weak, so drained. She felt as though someone was performing magic and used her psychological and mental health as its power source. She was only mildly aware of the depleting wind strength and slight increase in warmth. Flaragin was showing obvious signs of fatigue.

When they were a mile or so away from the eerie edge and the land flattened out considerably and began to show signs of green life; Leo dismounted and began to walk while Saoirse sat slump in the saddle. A little way ahead were some young boys climbing trees. They were laughing and throwing sticks at each other. Each one was daring the next to climb higher. When they drew nearer to them Leo called to them.

"Whoever gets to the ground fastest gets a free horse,"

All four of the boys began to race down. Their toes felt for branches below them, twigs scratched their skin and spiders fell on their heads as the webs were destroyed. One boy, the tallest had nearly reached the ground (and could almost taste success), when the boy above him lost his footing and fell landing painfully on his bum.

He stood up, rubbed his bum and squinted his eyes, "Which ones mine then?" he was eyeing up Flaragin with interest.

"You can have the dun but you have to do me one favour."

The boy looked at him trying to decide if he was being deceived, "Favours were not part of the bargain."

"This horse has a sore back, so you can't ride it for a few weeks. I need you to follow me to the cross roads just up the road and walk for a while on the path to the left. If you do that for me he's yours." The child was ecstatic.

"I live up there!" then he felt like he had said too much, "You aren't going to come back for it when it's better are you?"

"I give you my word he is yours."

All four of the boys ran up to the horse. The three losers were begging the boy to let them have the horse.

Leo walked with Flare to the cross roads then turned back the way they had come.

"Why did you give that horse away?" Saoirse asked.

"He has a deeper step because he's lame. His tracks will outlast Flare's. If anyone is following us they might split and follow his tracks. Also, he was slowing us down."

"Why are we going back the way we came?" Saoirse was building up to the question she really wanted to ask.

"I saw a cave that we can rest the night in, I don't want to risk resting in the open and if they haven't made it up that path by now, they won't make it in the dark." Leo was obviously tired as well. Saoirse thought it would be easier to get the truth out of him. It took energy to lie.

"Are you taking me to Troy?"

"I thought that question had already been answered. No I am not." He snapped

"Why did you come back for me?" She asked this one quieter as she was ashamed to admit even to herself that the answer mattered to her.

"Save your questions for when we rest."

It did not take long to find the cave. It was a tight fit at the entrance but the horse just squeezed in and it was more spacious further back. They went as far into the cave as they felt comfortable and the oddest thing happened. When their breath touched the walls it glowed a beautiful combination

201

of pinks and oranges. Leo wished he could describe it to Saoirse well enough to do it justice but he couldn't. It was just so illuminating. Leo didn't want to light a fire because he didn't want the smoke to give them away, but the cave walls seemed to not only glow but give off a gentle heat. Not enough to heat their bones but enough to take a bit of the chill from the air He gathered some rocks to try and disguise the entrance without making it too difficult to escape from. Leo gathered some grass for Flaragin to nibble on and to lay as a bed for Saoirse.

Flaragin was unsettled for a long time but eventually calmed enough to doze where she stood. She dreamt of her warm, straw filled stable, with a large bucket of water and a bountiful supply of hay ledge. Leo's thoughts weren't too different either. He lay very still in the hope that Saoirse would fall asleep and not ask any more questions at least until he was ready for them.

Alas it was not to be; Saoirse sat up straight waiting patiently for Leo to make a sound. He tried to make his breathing deeper and louder. Still she waited. She knew if she didn't get some answers her nightmares would return...

Eventually, Leo gave up and sat beside her staring everywhere but at her face. He looked at the many formations created by water dripping through the stone. The walls were moist as was the ground which made it very uncomfortable but the warmish glow certainly helped things. They had only moved a short way inside, compared to how far they could potentially go. It looked almost like a tunnel further back but it wasn't practical to move any further as Saoirse couldn't see and Flare was too large and spooky.

Then it arrived; the first question. Just when he thought he might be safe.

"Why did you come back for me?" The only emotion she allowed herself to show was curiosity.

"I promised you that I would."

"Why did you make that promise?"

"I couldn't live with myself if I allowed them to do to you what they planned to do to you."

"Why? You don't know me. You only invaded my dreams. I'm sure a lot of people have been attacked. In fact I know they have because I heard them. Why would you feel for me and not for them?"

"Because you are innocent, because I brought you here, because I thought that we had grown to be friends in the few months we shared together and mostly, because I knew what Troy had planned for you."

"What did he have planned for me?" Saoirse thought of all she had heard in the dungeon.

"I cannot and will not say. It is too awful for me to think of," Leo remembered his promise to Rad. Then he remembered the kiss and the look in her eye as he rode away. His heart dropped. What had happened to her? Would Troy discover what she had done? He felt bile rise in his stomach as he remembered the blood hit his face and the sound of the guard falling on top of his own guts.

"Why does Troy want to hurt me?"

"He sees you as the answer to a very big problem."

"That's not very informative."

"I cannot go into any more detail on that question."

With a bad temper rising to the surface she asked another question which had been nibbling like a mouse in her mind.

"Why are Troy and Alessandro fighting?"

"That's a very good question. I don't think anyone knows the real answer. There are many suggestions. Troy and Alessandro's fathers were brothers. Alessandro's father, your father too married your mother who was the Queen of Gandros. He was arrogant. I'm sorry but he was. He had power and he abused it, much like he abused your mother He sent out floods of men to conquer neutral lands. His reasoning was that he wanted to control them before they became a threat. Not to mention the taxes he would earn. They say Troy's father, your uncle wanted to put a stop to it and made a public stand. Shortly after that, he and his wife were murdered. Troy was a young boy then and unaware of what had happened. There was no strong evidence to prove it was the king but none to say otherwise.

Your mother was a good woman. It is said that she was part of the reason the two men fought. She insisted that she be allowed to raise Troy. After all, he was her nephew. I believe he finally gave in because he thought it would eliminate a threat. Anyway, when Troy grew a little older he began to ask questions and found out the suspicious circumstances surrounding his parent's death. Troy then took his revenge."

That was a lot of information to process. It created many more questions.

"You mean Troy is my cousin?" she could hardly spit the words from her tongue, "My own cousin wants to hurt me?" this was so painful to digest, "My father is a killer, He is the cause of all this, I am the daughter of a killer, I have the blood of a power hungry, villain running through my veins, Did Troy kill them? Both of them?"

"Yes." A short response to a long quizzical rant.

"Why both of them? Why my mother?" She was shaking her head and kept closing her eyes as though that would protect her.

"She allowed it to happen, I suppose. Your mother, in my opinion did not deserve to die, but being idle is just as much a sin as the sin itself, He was much older than her and born into a well-known, prosperous family, he had blood connections to the Queen of another country, I can't remember which, over to the east I think, your mother's family told her to behave and do as she was told, and she did. It is customary to marry the first born of the chosen family. I think."

"You gave your loyalty to the man that killed a good, decent woman, My Mother." She was disgusted and wanted to get away from him.

Leo had only recently come to think of his actions in that light, He had always viewed her as Alessandros mother, the woman who stood by a murderer and raised one as well. What had he done? He hated Alessandro for not helping his mother, what then does Saoirse think of him. He aided the man who made her an orphan. He was truly ashamed of himself.

"You have no idea of the depth in which my apology originates, I promise that I will do all that I can to right my wrong. My conscience attacks me constantly; I am ashamed of the man I have become." It was the truth, and he meant it all.

"Why did you go to him? Why did you choose him?"

"At the time, I believed it to be a good reason."

"What was that reason?"

"Please can we rest now, we have a long day tomorrow, when we wake I will answer more. Now I really do need to rest." He laid his head down to rest and used his arm as a pillow.

Saoirse was silent for a short time but then quietly asked Leo, "Leo? Leo I'm so cold. Can you come a little closer please? I'm worried I'll roll and fall of a ledge or something." She was ashamed to ask but was genuinely concerned she would cause herself harm.

Leo shuffled closer to her and pulled her to him and wrapped his arms around her. It was uncomfortably intimate but after a while it felt more like safety, security. Safety; with Leo! How ridiculous she thought. Saoirse had to remind herself not to allow herself to trust him yet. He had not proven he was not out to do her more harm. It could still be a trick. His strong arms seemed to sense what she was thinking and Leo instinctively squeezed her tighter while he slept. Saoirse in turn wrapped her legs around his and held his arm with hers. Their breathing synced up and they both fell into a surprising deep dream filled sleep. In that moment she could temporarily forget that he had failed her. She felt safe. She felt at home in his arms if even for that brief frozen moment.

Chapter Twenty

Leo was first to awake. He unblocked enough of the exit to slip through and went in search of berries, roots and eggs, He filled his saddle bags and even managed to acquire some bread that was cooling on a windowsill, he felt bad but survival came first.

When he came back Saoirse was still asleep, He was glad of that because he didn't know how she would react to waking up and only hearing the horse's breath beside her.

He calmly poked her awake and handed her a piece of bread which she devoured ravenously.

"Where are we going?"

"We are going to find Alessandro and the Hoggron Xzenny tribe." As they spoke he unblocked the way out completely and began to saddle Flaragin."

"Haven't you been searching for them for over a decade now?"

"Yes, but now we have an idea where the Hoggron Xzenny tribe are hiding."

"Do you think Alessandro is with them?" Saoirse truly wanted to meet her brother.

"I couldn't say I suppose it could be possible that he is searching for them as well, they have both managed to work in secret and the world is not that big, so it is plausible. Are you ready?"

"Ready for what exactly?"

"To mount Flaragin."

"I am not riding again, I will walk." She backed up tight against the wall.

"You will be too slow on foot; you know it makes sense, so walk forward and I will throw you up."

"I will fall for sure, how will that make us move faster?" Saoirse felt along the wall towards the wind.

"I know that it must have been petrifying for you but we will walk and I will help you get the feel of the horse so you are not terrified. It won't be that awful."

"Have you ever flown blind folded?"

Leo laughed and grabbed her hand.

"Trust me on this." Leo felt guilty at asking her to trust him after all he had done. Saoirse was surprised that she was considering trusting him, especially so soon after he betrayed her trust.

"If I fall, I will learn to curse you."

"That's a fair deal."

He pulled her forward and placed her hand at the horse's chest.

"Feel her breathing; she is calm now you see?"

He brought her to Flares head.

"Hold out your hand and hold it flat," she did as she was told and Flare started to lick her hand.

"She's licking the salt off your hand," he laughed as Saoirse flinched, "Now gently blow on her nose, barely more than a breath,"

She did and Flare breathed on her in return, "You see your friends now. It's all about reading her signs and you don't have to be able to see to do that. If her heart beats too fast rub her neck and talk to her gently. If she starts to prance you just keep your back straight, your heels down and breathe; if you forget how to breathe the sing a song. Unless we are trying to hide,"

Saoirse nodded nervously. She went as stiff as a plank of wood when Leo placed his hands around her waist and lifted her up into the saddle.

"Keep your legs down and try to wrap them around her as best you can. Sit up straight and you will have a better balance. You can hold on to the front of the saddle for support and keep your heels down." He reminded her, "And try to relax,"

They started to walk.

"If you feel her muscles moving, then try to go to that rhythm."

Saoirse tried to calm down and let her body move with the horse; Leo walked at the head of the horse and kept her steady.

"So how do you plan to find the Hoggron Xzenny tribe?"

"I have a theory that I plan to test when we rest later in the day. As you may know, I'm a dream dropper,"

"Really? I never noticed," Saoirse interrupted sarcastically.

"I can travel into dreams of anyone I like, I just need to concentrate," Leo decided to ignore her outburst, "I have never managed to reach Alessandro, so it is possible that he has protection from me, I know that the Hoggron Xzenny Tribe are located somewhere in the Shay loo Forest. I want to dream drop into the trees."

"Trees? Is that possible?" Saoirse was not overly optimistic.

Leo picked a leaf from the nearest tree and turned it upside. He prised Saoirse's hand off the saddle.

"Do you feel the veins?"

"I know what a leaf feels like." She snapped as she snatched her hand back and put it safely back where it belonged.

"Sorry, but you see trees have veins, they breath and they reproduce. They have an energy all to themselves, it is a logical assumption that they are alive, the fact that they are stationary and do not communicate could suggest that they are constantly in a dream state. I know it doesn't make any sense to you, but please keep your mind open."

"Are we going to Shayloo Forest now?"

"We are taking a route that I hope will not be easy to track."

"Does that mean it is not easy to travel on as well?"

"It is not the easiest route. Then again, no way of travel is guaranteed safe."

Saoirse was worried by his response, but his lack of fear gave her hope. She managed to relax and was not as tense as she had been, that however did not stop her from holding on as though her life depended on it, which it probably did,

They walked without speech for some time, until Leo suggested they stop so that he could try out his theory and have something to eat, both Flaragin and Saoirse were glad of the break, Saoirse's legs were aching and she felt as though her hands had grown into the saddle. It was difficult for her to lift her leg and let go, even with Leo's help. As her feet touched the ground her knees could not accept her weight and she fell backwards into waiting arms.

"It can be difficult riding for hours when you are not accustomed to it. Don't worry it won't always hurt this much." His voice was soft and his touch gentle. He took Saoirse's hand and led her to a rock.

Saoirse did not know it, but they were surrounded by rock infested fields, the grass was lacking in nutrients and showed it in its colour even though there were several small streams to nourish it, there were patches of ground that turned into marsh and buzzards were plentiful, though relatively quiet as many were busy with the process of consuming the meat of the carcasses that littered the fields.

Leo filled their water flasks from a small trickle of water that was filtering through some tight formations of rocks. It looked clear enough.

He looked forward on their trail and wondered if Saoirse could cope, she could not ride the entire way, and it would get very cold. The rocky path lead quite far up the mountain, it would be a great challenge.

"I'm sorry about the food; there isn't much fresh food on offer. I'll hunt later, I'm going to try to dream drop now so don't be concerned at my shallow breaths, I won't hear you if you talk, not this time."

"Alright." What she really wanted to say was; what in the name of good health do I do if someone attacks?

"I can see you are frightened, but for now we are as safe as we are ever going to get." Saoirse could picture his smile.

"You're a bad liar Leo," she teased, "And I'm not afraid. Don't presume that because I'm female I'm afraid,"

"No I assume that you would be afraid because you are in a strange world surrounded by enemies and you have no idea where to go or what to do and if I should die while dream dropping you really would be rather stuck wouldn't you?"

"You forget Leo Dovinpoir I am the daughter of a psychopath, the cousin to a warmonger and sister to a man who has evaded capture by the notorious dream dropper. I am both Saoirse Slamina and Sarah Hawthorne, and I will not be beaten just because you decide to get yourself killed. I may stumble a little but I kick ass!" How dare he point out her predicament? She knew full well she would be in very deep hot water if he left her defenceless but that was no need for him to point it out; even in jest.

"You're right of course your highness, Princess Saoirse. How could a peasant such as myself hope to serve one as great as you?" At that he started to circle her as he talked, "You are so superior. You have no need for me. You can escape any attack," at that he jumped on her from behind but Saoirse had been prepared and rolled to the side, leaving him to face plant the dirt.

"Not any attack, but I can out smart you! What was it you had said? Oh yes. It's all about reading the signs. You don't have to see to read them. It works on people as well as horses Leo. Listen for the breathing, the footsteps and the direction of the voice. I'm a quick study,"

"Well, um, I'm glad you were listening to my advice. I should get to work," He was both embarrassed and impressed. His face reddened at Saoirse's laughter, so he moved away from her and started to concentrate on the job at hand.

Leo pictured what he remembered of Shayloo Forest and then homed in on a tree and tried to concentrate on the veins of the leaves. He felt the texture, the moisture and tried to imagine a trees breath.

Eventually, the vision began to form. It was as though he was seeing from many eyes, like a fly. There were no colours, just black and white. He was being moved by a weak breeze. he could feel insects crawling all over him, birds breaking twigs and building a home for themselves, caterpillars eating his leaves, his eyes, he was unnerved by the sensation caused by his roots sucking up water and nutrients. Usually when he entered a dream, he was an observer but this time he was the tree.

He did appreciate the ability to feel every tiny movement in the ground, sounds of weary voices resounded in his ears. He seemed to hear through vibrations hitting his entire body. When Leo visited people's dreams he was himself because he could blend into their experiences, now he had moulded his soul into that of a tree, integrating with them but not the active world.

"I don't know what he expects us to find, it's not as if they are going to pop out and say hello. I guess you found us. We will do whatever you ask of us."

These were Troy's men; they were searching for the Hoggron Xzenny. It worked he could watch them and they would be completely unaware, Leo was delighted and rushed back to his own mind to tell Saoirse.

He leapt up and startled her by giving her an energetic and unexpected hug; he pulled her into a standing position and hugged her again.

"Am I to assume it worked?" taken aback, but otherwise delighted Saoirse laughed.

"I've never seen like that before, it was as though I actually was the tree, not just visiting, it was truly fascinating. I saw one of Troy's search parties, they are small."

"Every time we rest I will dream drop into a different part of the forest, that way we can search without being in a major risk, I can plan our path before we get there, I will show you in your dreams where we are heading, not now of course, when we stop to sleep. So let me get us some food to eat and more water to drink. Then I will put you back on Flaragin and we shall march onwards."

His happiness was infectious and after their small meal they started off again with a spring in their step.

Saoirse quickly became accustomed to the rhythm of the horses stride, there were times, when she did not feel Leo's eyes on her, that she lifted her hands from the saddle and felt a rush of adrenaline, it was very exciting to remain unsupported, yet balanced sitting on another living creature, she was trusting her safety, not just with Leo but with this animal that had a mind of its own, if it so desired she could be on the ground faster than a shark could turn.

Leo advised her to lean forward when they were travelling up a hill, it seemed to Saoirse that they were constantly travelling further up, it seemed to be getting colder, as though she would soon have icicles on the end of her nose, she did not complain, but her silence was more of a signal of her discomfort than her voice could have been.

"Saoirse, lets rest here for a bit, It's going to get a lot colder and wetter from here on, so I want to fill our clothes with dry leaves to try to insulate ourselves - I also think that you should try to sleep. I can show you where we are going; this will be the last warmish place to sleep for a few days at least."

Saoirse did not say a word; she simply threw her leg over Flaragin hind quarters and gently slid down into Leo's arms, he stood behind her and once again Saoirse's breath stopped as his breath warmed her neck.

She turned herself around and Leo loosened his grip slightly, she placed her head on his chest and felt his body lean backwards slightly as he took a deep breath, she brought her arms up to her head and began to weep.

"I'm so scared Leo, I really am. I lied before"

He hugged her tight and rested his chin on her cushioned head.

"I know that this is my fault, I made a terrible mistake, but right now I know what I must do, I want to protect you, and I will, I am so sorry, I really truly am."

As he held her his feelings grew to a higher level, he wasn't sure if he just wanted to protect her to put right a wrong, he really cared for her, he had to fight back tears, he thought of Rad and the kiss, then thought of Saoirse, he held her close until she stopped crying, he smelt her hair and took in every one of her features, all he could think of was what Troy had planned for her, would Alessandro behave any better? How could he ensure a safe secure future for her? The fact was he couldn't, he didn't even know if he could keep her alive, it was he who brought her into this and he couldn't send her back to safe ignorance.

"Please forgive me."

"I forgive you Leo, but I hate you just as much as I don't want you to go."

"I am nailed to your side, I am going nowhere."

They hugged for a few more minutes until Leo broke his trance and told her to lie down and sleep. He guided her to a safe spot below a large tree and watched as her breathing slowed, he placed the saddle cloth over her shivering body and talked to Flaragin for a short while.

When Saoirse fell asleep she was transported to a library in the palace of her first visit. The beaten woman was there talking to what appeared to be her shadow.

"You can hide the truth in the shadow realm? He won't find it? I need to know that the truth will get out when the time is right. I have written it all. Everything I have learned."

She handed the book to her shadow and it split in two and burst through the book shelves with the book. There was a brief blast of grey but then it was gone. The beaten woman dressed today in Red and she had a cheeky smile. That smile spoke of potential revenge. Then the woman twirled an almost carefree twirl and stared straight through Saoirse and said, "The truth will always be spoken. I will make sure of it. No one will hurt my people," and the beaten woman walked straight through Saoirse and out the door and her figure dispersed into the air. Saoirse thought about telling Leo about the beaten woman. Was she also some form of dream dropper? Or a memory? Or a ghost of some sort? She decided to wait until she knew she could trust Leo completely before she told him about her.

Leo thought of visiting Rad to try to figure out how he felt about her but knew it would be too early and she would not be asleep, instead, he decided to visit another section of Shayloo Forest, his hunt was fruitless.

When he went into Saoirse's dream the hurricane was over and there was just a patter of rain, he found her in the main palace staring at the paintings.

"Are these people my family?" It had taken Saoirse a while to realize this.

"Yes, they are." Leo came and stood beside her, he had to knot his hands together behind his back to stop them from wrapping around Saoirse.

"Which one is my mother?"

"Your mother and father are at the top of the stairs along with your brother, your mothers portrait was painted when she was eighteen, and then a couple painting was done on her wedding day. That involved a lot of standing around when I'm sure they had other things they wanted to do.," Leo stifled a laugh.

They walked side by side up the marble stairs, until Leo suddenly stopped and stepped behind her, he covered her eyes with his hands and she reached up with hers to pull them away.

"No let me reveal them to you," he could feel the muscles in her face pull into a smile.

They walked step by step, his left leg pushed hers forward, then her right led his. He was glad he could make her happy this way.

"Miss Saoirse Slamina, I am proud to present her majesty the Queen Lady Slamina, Lord Slamina and Master Alessandro Slamina, your immediate family." He slowly removed his hands to reveal a sight that Saoirse had seen before, but was looking at with fresh eyes.

Saoirse thought they were a beautiful family, all of them had long curly hair, her mother's hair was a vibrant red and her eyes were a strong green. She had soft features and a feminine frame she was the beaten woman. The portrait made her look so happy. Her father on the other hand looked strong, he had a rather large red nose and dark hair, his eyes were a blue, but the black pupil seemed larger and quite hypnotic. He was the angry violent man from her dreams. He was the man that beats her mother. Saoirse wondered if the artist had exaggerated the evil look of her father, but her brother was just the same, he seemed to be a younger version of his father; they even smiled the same, but with his mothers eyes Saoirse wondered did he take after their mother or their father.

"Your mother's parents are the two before them, and the two before them are your mother's grandparents. Her grandfather died protecting her grandmother from thieves, He was quite young at the time and he won the battle but died later on in his bed, your grandmother died less than a month later. It was said she proclaimed to all the servants that she refused to live another day without her partner. That night she was found dead in her bed, hands on her heart, your grandmother then had to take the throne at the age of fourteen."

Saoirse looked at her great-grandparents; her grandmother had red hair, green eyes and high cheek bones. She looked as though she was not the sort of woman you would want to infuriate, but had an obvious loving quality that glowed through her eyes and skin. Her grandfather seemed to be a smaller build than her father, but still had good muscle formation; he had mild green eyes and fair hair.

"I can't believe I'm never going to meet them," she looked away from the painting with a heavy heart ache.

Leo put his hand on her back and said, "I'll find Alessandro for you; he can tell you all about them."

"I hope we find him soon, where is my uncle? You said Troy was my cousin, where are their paintings?"

"Usually they only painted those who were to take on the throne or who married them, so I don't know if there is one of him."

"Leo."

"Yes."

"I'm waking up."

"But I need to show you the way."

"I can hear the world out there and it's grabbing me back, you'll just have to continue to guide me."

When Saoirse fully woke up Leo was already there, he was sitting in front of her, not looking very happy.

"You didn't sleep very long."

She said nothing and didn't move while Leo saddled up.

"There is a stack of leaves slightly to your left; I want you to fill your clothes with them.

Saoirse did as she was told and asked no questions.

Before long, they were knee deep in snow and going blindly forward into strong winds and sharp blizzards, Flaragin was as always obedient and any attempt at talking by either Leo or Saoirse was stifled by a mouthful of falling frozen water.

They travelled in these conditions deep into the night; they had to keep moving because if they stopped they would be buried in their sleep and die of exposure to extreme cold.

When their limbs were on the verge of falling off, Leo began to feel the side of the mountain, there had to be a cave somewhere, the temperature of this region changes so dramatically it had to have an effect on the rocks.

After two more hours he found it, the bottom half was blocked with ice and snow, his vision was obscured but once he had helped Saoirse dismount they went in and finally he could hear his thoughts again.

The tunnel led to a larger, airy, rocky, clearing with sharp icicles decorating the ceiling, the ground had a thin layer of ice. Leo decided it would be safer not to climb down into enclosure for many reasons, it would not be much warmer, Saoirse might trip and cause the ice to break and Flaragin could not make it down without jumping.

They slept huddled together, all of them exhausted. Leo did not even have the energy to look ahead or visit Rad, their breaths rose and froze to the ceiling. Leo wrapped himself around Saoirse, she did not protest, her hands were hidden under her armpits as they were turning blue, they were shivering uncontrollably. This cave had the same effect as the other cave they had rested in. When their breath touched the walls it glowed pink and orange. Leo wondered if perhaps the caves were connected. A large part of him wanted to go exploring and see if they were linked but he couldn't leave Saoirse and it was too darn cold.

The night eventually passed and when the sun rose the heat could almost be felt, the light on the snow, as they emerged back into the wild, nearly blinded Leo he had to keep his eyes squinted.

"We are on level ground for a while, so it would probably be a good idea if you walked for a bit, the weather can change from one extreme to the next here in an hour. There can be a sweltering heat wave one moment then a monstrous snow storm the next."

"May I have a drink of water?" What she really wanted was a large Sunday roast with a glass of wine.

"Best to wait as long as you can, we don't have much left."

"What about the snow? Can we not melt it? There is a lot, enough to water an army."

"We cannot, if you think you are cold now it will be even worse if you consume the snow and we cannot light a fire to melt it, we will begin our descent before long, there will soon be grass between our toes once more."

Leo was right; they did start to walk down hill, after three agonising days, of pushing themselves to the limit, the air became so thin no matter how many breaths Saoirse took, she was still lacking in oxygen, she felt light headed, stumbled repeatedly bruised her face from falling and came close to fainting on numerous occasions.

"It's better than being dead," she kept telling herself. "Better than where I was, better then where Leo sent me," she was so conflicted about Leo. she forced herself to concentrate on her steps, but then maybe that was why Leo was making her walk, so that she wouldn't think of what he could be planning, why would he save her just to kill her, maybe he found a higher bidder, or maybe he genuinely felt guilty and wanted to make right what he had done.

It was no less than three and a half days before the temperature began to rise, the air gradually became breathable once more, not long after that Saoirse felt the moist grass, not much of it was present, but soon they would be fighting through waist high blades.

"It is a difficult descent, but after this we can rest. I mean a proper rest, with real sleep at last, do you think you would prefer to walk down or ride down? I will have to lead Flaragin anyway, so if you feel confident in your balance perhaps it would be best."

"I will try to ride; I am aching all over."

"You will ache more should you fall, hold on with your life."

Saoirse mounted and was filled once more with the dread she had hoped to escape.

The sight in front of her was unbelievable, even if she could not see it, she smelt the freshness of the air, she could hear the call of the eagle and the flight of the hawk, wild Scallings were running around, hovering just that little bit above the ground, making a sound that was truly unique to their species. When the grass was more abundant, Saoirse could almost feel the rabbits burrowing beneath her, the sky was clear and the clouds were no more than a whisper, all seemed calm, but was it only an illusion?

Saoirse was nearly unseated more than once, but quickly learnt how to predict when Flaragin was about to jump, or pick up the pace. She wondered if riding a horse would be any more enjoyable if she could see.

Chapter Twenty-One

When they reached level ground, Saoirse slid off the horse and lay down, she felt so weak, so exhausted, so very, very unsure of anything.

"You cannot sleep here; we are in an open area, no protection from the elements of our enemies."

"Why did you ask me to dismount then?" Saoirse's irritation shinned strong in her voice, lack of sleep was making her cranky.

"I have a task to do that may take some time."

"What task? What are you doing? What is that noise?"

"I really do not think you would feel comfortable knowing what I am doing."

"Leo, I demand you tell me what you are doing. It just isn't fair to do things in front of me knowing full well I cannot see." She began to move towards Leo, touching the ground to guide her.

"Alright, please stop there, soon there will be a terrible smell that you will want to flee from, there is a mound of stones here which means that there is someone buried beneath it, there are a strange tribe that are known to roam this area and they bury their dead with weapons."

"You mean to say you are grave robbing, Leo that is unforgiveable, I cannot allow you to do this, I will not be part of it."

"If I don't do this we are vulnerable when attacked, when, Saoirse not IF, let me do this or we will die." I cannot defend without weapons, good weapons; you also need to be armed."

Saoirse refused to agree, but also refrained from disagreeing.

The smell of decomposing flesh rose slowly at first, and then seemed to be released onto Saoirse faster than a dragon's strike. She shuffled backwards, tears stinging her eyes, her nostrils were being burnt and her clothes ripped as she slid her behind across a rock.

"Right, I've got what we need, so let's go." Leo touched Saoirse's arm and she pulled it away from him,

"You have to cover him up again, say some kind of prayer or apology."

"We have been out in the open long enough, and the buzzards need to eat as well."

"This is completely disrespectful; I'll cover him up if you won't."

Saoirse barely moved when Leo grabbed her around the waist and threw her over his shoulder.

"You don't have much of a choice! Now hold your tongue unless you want to attract an attack."

Saoirse swore at him and hit him on the head, to her great disgust he just laughed.

It was a short walk to a leaf littered sanctuary, there were several bee hives buzzing with activity, there were strange grey squirrels flying from branch to branch, a skunk walked straight past Saoirse and a badger behind her. Some distance away, there was a trumpet of the forest elephant, an acknowledgement that a vast water supply was nearby, a small brightly coloured bird hopped down several branches to see who the new arrivals were. He had curious eyes and puffed out his feathers making him look like a stray ball of wool.

Leo eventually set Saoirse down and lit a small fire; they drank some water and ate a little food.

"I'll go hunting again shortly," Leo proclaimed confidently.

Saoirse ignored him.

"Saoirse, I am sorry, but this is about survival." He slowly moved closer to her.

She continued to ignore him; they sat without talking while Leo examined the weaponry.

"There are some unusual designs on the shield and dagger; would you like me to describe them to you?

Silence prevailed.

"Well I'll tell you anyway, there is a cross with four equal sides, at the end of the horizontal line it turns into a wavy line, on the inside of each curve there is a circle, seven on each side. As for the vertical the straight line extends and nine solid circles are placed evenly spaced, then on the end of the lines before the circles a line is drawn to join up each of the sections to form a right angle triangle, four in total. Inside each triangle is a symbol for an earthly element. I would love to know what it represents."

"Perhaps we may enlighten you."

Saoirse felt a blade at her throat and screamed hysterically, her feeble attempt at an escape caused the knife to cut her.

"Stay calm Sarah, it'll all be ok."

"Ever the optimist Leo."

"I'm just that good. I am great and realistic and modest."

"Seriously, are you trying to make me laugh when I have a knife to my throat?"

"Well would you prefer I mock you for not reading the signs?"

"Silence. You desecrated the grave of our chief, you disturbed his spirit. He says you now must die."

"You ass, Leo! What did I tell you? Say a prayer! Cover him up. No Sarah, we have no time Sarah. I know best Sarah. This is survival Sarah. We need to save time! How much time do u think our death will use up you absolute mule!"

"Even a genius has to get a few things wrong."

"You irresponsible, disrespectful, narcissist!"

"Come on now; keep talking like that and I won't save your life, again."

"You keep risking my life Leo!"

As they argued the tribesmen bound their hands and feet and then tied them to a large stick so they were swinging from the stick as the tribesmen carried them.

"Be thankful you can't see the view. The leather strips from their skirt doesn't cover up much. I'm telling you Sarah there is a lot of flesh showing. It's so undignified."

"So is being tied to a branch upside down and being carried to your death. Get your priorities straight!"

They continued to argue as they were carried for miles. Their joints were aching and their throats were becoming hoarse but Leo wanted to keep Saoirse angry. The longer she was mad at him the less time she would be able to think about how frightened she really was. You never completely lose the fear from living a life like this but if the only life you can remember is a sheltered family life, with very few life threatening events, it can take a while to become accustomed to the fear and be able to function.

"And you can't cook at all. There was no flavour in that crap you tried to feed me. Was it even real meat? Was it

225

even cooked right! Leo I can smell burning. Why can I smell burning? Where are we?"

They had reached the tribesmen's campsite. It was an impressive sight. There were hammocks in the trees with the branches from the trees tied to provide shelter. There were wooden huts for the more important people and animal skin tents for others. There were various devises that Leo suspected were for punishment. One was a deep grave with men and women standing at the ready with shovels and angry faces. Another torture devise was a strong wooden cage wrapped in unbreakable plaited vines suspended over a lake. There was also a platform for being burned at a stake and a large platform high above the trees that Leo couldn't quite see what was on it. Every face was directed towards them and they all looked angry.

They came to a halt in the centre of the circle around which all the people had gathered. A chief came up to Leo with a large coloured feather and waved it over his face. The feather dissolved into water and splashed on Leos face.

"You are controlled by the element of water. You have lived your life by the way of water therefore your death shall be by water."

"Leo, you stubborn mule what is going on? What does he mean? Will you tell him that you are sorry or something? Anything!"

The chief then moved on to Saoirse with another feather he waved it over her face and the feather turned to ash that fell on Saoirse's face.

"You are a woman of fire, now as punishment you shall burn."

Suddenly, both were surrounded and were overpowered. Saoirse was tied to the platform of fire and Leo was thrown in the water cage.

"Leo use magic. Magic is real; you told me it was, so use it."

"I don't know any magic."

"You can trespass in people's dreams but you can't untie a knot."

"It's not as simple as hocus pocus open knot us. You need to study magic or you can really mess things up."

A small child picked up a burning log from the camp fire and brought it to the chief. It must have been a great honour as the child looked very proud. The chief threw the log onto the platform that Saoirse was trapped on and passionately cast a spell to increase the speed that the flames spread. He then waved his hand and muttered more words as Leo's cage plummeted into the water.

"I am Saoirse Slamina. I have not studied magic but I stand here fighting my fear and I call to my brother to find me. Alessandro I am here. Save me brother. I have power in me I know it, but I don't know the words."

The thunder of hooves drowned out Saoirse's screams.

"The word is please sister. I'm glad your home."

Chapter Twenty-Two

Alessandro sitting astride his noble steed jumped through the flames bringing with him a wave of water. Saoirse was never so happy to be soaked through to the skin. She laughed and screamed with joy.

"Leo. Please save Leo. He's in a cage near water."

"He already did," Leo whispered as he untied the knots that restrained her, "Come on."

"We can't leave him. We have to fight as well."

"Saoirse you can't see your enemy." Once again Saoirse was thrown over Leos shoulder and carried to Flaragin. They both mounted and galloped off.

"Oh Leo he found us. How did he find us? Isn't it amazing?"

"He must have already been on our trail. You didn't summon him if that's what you think. He probably could have helped sooner."

"Leo, don't be jealous because you're not the hero this time." She hugged him close both soaking wet and glad to be alive. She didn't even remember to be afraid of ridding.

They kept moving but eventually slowed to a walk and Alessandro and his men caught up with them. That was when the fear set in. What would they do to Leo? He was their enemy. What would her brother think of her? Did he want to be part of her life? Well he did just jump through flames for her. That's bound to be on the plus side. Then again, maybe he won't be happy about having to save her and she was already a burden.

"Artur take Saoirse on your horse with you. Just encase the boy gets second thoughts."

"I brought her this far, what exactly do you think I'm going to do?"

"I have not had the time to assess your madness; my job now is to ensure my sister does not suffer at your hands again."

"No one hurts Leo! Promise me or I won't get off this horse." Saoirse looked in the direction she thought Alessandro was riding.

"He won't be hurt, yet."

The threat was obvious. That was all Alessandro said for the next four hours they travelled. After all, what could he say she was back too soon; much too soon. Thalious had failed him. Saoirse dismounted Flare and was helped onto another much taller horse by a man much taller than Leo. He was gentle and polite. He tried numerous times to make small talk then he reverted to silence for a few hours until he could bare it no more.

"For a woman with so much to say you're very quiet." A strange voice invaded Saoirse's thoughts.

"What gives you the impression I have a lot to say?"

"You have been gone ten years."

"That doesn't mean I have a lot to say, perhaps just a lot to ask."

"Well then why don't you ask me?"

"I don't know who you are."

"Well I am Artur. I train the horses, or I should say that I train the people who ride the horses."

"So you can teach me to ride properly?"

"I can try. I've never failed yet."

"And you can answer my questions?

"I can try," He smiled. He had not expected Saoirse to be like this. She was quite attractive and confident despite all her current woes.

"O.K. Question one. What's my brother like?" She smiled but there was a sadness that she could not hide.

"He's our king. He can fight like a bear, but with the stealth of a cheetah. He's a quiet man, thinks before he speaks. Sometimes has an outburst of anger but not often. He is tall, green eyes, dark hair. He can handle a horse almost as well as I can, and he was very happy to learn his baby sister was alive and on her way home."

"You're a fan then," she laughed, "Did he tell you he was happy to find me?"

"Not in words but I can tell."

They continued to talk with Leo watching nearby, who was in turn being watched closely by Alessandro. They trekked for three days and seemed to cover the same ground over and over again. Saoirse hadn't been able to sleep properly as they didn't stop for long. She just seemed to drift off to sleep when someone came and shook her awake telling her to move on. Leo had no idea where they were going, though he had been keeping track of their journey and was confident he could find his way back. Leo knew they had looped around and back tracked, it was a way to confuse him, to make him vulnerable, less of a threat. They were wrong.

"Leave the horses to graze. We go by foot from here." Saoirse heard Alessandro's orders but she had still not spoken to him. She was also still petrified of dismounting, even with Artur's tutoring. She was determined to be independent, not to be a burden on anyone. She leant forward feeling the horses neck and took both her feet out of the stirrups. She tried to throw her leg over but lost her nerve and balanced awkwardly. She was so stiff and cold and tired.

"Your nearly there," a calm voice encourages her. Artur had barely left her side these past few days. "Keep moving your leg across. That's it. Now drop down and bend your knees." Saoirse fell backwards into Artur's arms.

"I can help her from here." Leo had arrived and he sounded angry. He wasn't getting the best treatment and she wished she could make it easier for him.

"I think you've helped enough Leo."

"I taught her to ride!" he retorted feebly.

"Then care for the horse and I'll take care of Saoirse." he threw the reins at Leo with a look of disgust and took Saoirse's elbow.

"Should we not all go together? If we are going to the same place?" Saoirse didn't want to leave Leo alone. She needed him to stay close so she could at least feel as though she was protecting him.

"I'm sure Leo will be too busy with his horse."

"It won't take too long to water her and rub her down. Perhaps Saoirse would like to help me since Flare has been so good to her. What do you think Saoirse?"

"I'd like to thank her Artur. Do you mind? She is an amazing animal."

"Well I suppose many hands make light work. I have a spare cloth in my saddle bag."

Flare had never been so pampered. Her tack was removed and well hidden. She had three pairs of hands wipe her down and even got her mane and tail combed. She was checked over for cuts and heat. Saoirse talked to Flare and thanked her for her hard work and patience. Leo laughed at her until he noticed that Artur wasn't. So he kept quiet.

"We are not too far from the Hoggron Xzenny. It's about an hour's walk, then a short swim and then you will finally have a proper night's sleep. My guess is you would really like that," Artur laughed, "I know I've been dreaming of it."

"It's the only thing I can think of. Hold on, swim? Why swim? No one said anything about swimming."

"It's nothing to worry about. I'll help you if you get into trouble. You have my word."

"And I'll be there as well encase he.... Gets distracted," Leo and Artur glared at each other.

"I'm not in the habit of putting young women in danger. Are you?" Artur spat on the ground.

"I protect my own." Leo snarled.

"Then what are you doing here?"

"Perhaps we should keep walking." Saoirse was feeling uncomfortable and didn't know how to fix it. They really hate Leo, and the feeling seems to be mutual. This is not good, Saoirse thought, not good at all.

"This way, Saoirse," Artur took Saoirse's arm and started to walk. Leo was fuming but seeing how he didn't know the way, there was nothing he could do. He jogged to catch up and looked at Saoirse's free hand. Should he take her hand? Arthur had her arm and she seemed okay with that, but a hand is different. Maybe she wanted Arthur to take her hand and not him.

"Leo?" Saoirse stretched out her arm to make sure he was there. Almost instinctively he took her hand. Their fingers intertwined and then Saoirse stopped. She gasped. Leo let go, not sure what happened.

He had no idea that Saoirse had just had a flash of sight. She saw the tall trees whose branches and leaves were dancing in the light breeze. She saw the sun shining with all its might and how it didn't reach everywhere because some of the trees were so thick they cast impenetrable shadows. She saw butterflies and insects and even a snake slither rapidly away into the taller grass that was almost yellow.

"What's wrong, Saoirse?" they both asked in unison.

"Nothing, sorry. Just realised I might get to speak to my brother soon and I got a little nervous." She grabbed both their hands and marched off trying to pretend to be confident. It had been amazing. An electric shock to her brain and eyes and dare she say it, her heart. She was not willing to analyse it yet. It was a brief flash but then it was gone.

"Artur, Can you tell me what the entrance to the Hoggron Xzenny looks like and what will happen when we get there? Please."

With a cautious look at Leo, which caused Leo to roll his eyes Artur began.

"Soon you will be able to hear a very large waterfall. Less than a mile downstream from the bottom of the falls the river splits into three. Each section is wide and deep and the current can be strong. From the side we are approaching from, we will emerge from colourful woodland. The leaves on some of the trees are copper, all year round, others are green and there are many blossoms of various shades of red, purple and yellow. Some of the petals fall into the river and decorate it, making it seem so tranquil. There are bushes with fruit and berries, some are edible and some aren't. I tend to watch which ones the birds eat. When we reach where the river splits, a member of the Hoggron Xzenny guard will speak with Alessandro and any newcomers to evaluate their loyalty."

"How will they know we have arrived? Can they see us?"

"They control a type of bird. It's called a claih. They are mainly white with an orange eye and a black beak. It has feathers at the side of its head almost to the ears that are black and their tail feathers alternate white and black which is how they send signals. They can hide all the white feathers or all the black or make the black feathers thicker. They are in the trees around us and will send word of our arrival to the Hoggron Xzenny.

It was not long before the sound of the wild river and raging waterfall reached the ears of the weary travellers and they all quickened their pace. Alessandro had not spoken to Saoirse since their first meeting, but he watched her intently. Trying to figure out how to ensure she didn't die. Thalious had truly let him down. How was he unaware of the severity of the situation?

When they reached their destination, it was just as Artur had described. There was a tall almost sickly thin man with skin so pale it was almost transparent. It was possible to see the blood flowing and the nerves twitching. His face and posture were expressionless.

Alessandro stood with one foot in the shallows of the water and one on the land as he talked to the guard, who was standing on the mound of earth between the first split in the river.

"This might take a while. We should rest over here by a tree." Artur guided her to a shaded spot. Saoirse wasn't sure if she was being paranoid or not but she thought she was being taken away so she couldn't hear what Alessandro was saying. "Rest for a while. We will come and get you when we are ready."

Leo sat next to Saoirse and folded his arms and legs, silently daring Artur to tell him to leave. It began to get uncomfortably warm, even in the shade. The smell of the flowers was so relaxing. The heat comforting, Leo tried to stay awake but it was a fruitless battle. He drifted off without noticing.

His dream was black and white. It was just his home as an infant. He saw his mother on a rocking chair; she was holding his infant self close to her. She was staring out to the mountains, she was sad but gaining comfort from her child. Leo had become increasingly aware of a strange presence in his dreams. He wasn't sure if it was paranoia, but what if Troy had found a way into people's dreams. There were other ways apart from being a dream dropper. There were people who possessed strong magic and dream pools, if they were real. There was also the possibility of another dream dropper. It was not a wise move to get rid of an asset such as Leo was to Troy unless you had a backup, some kind of protection. What was his plan? "I know someone is here. Show yourself! I am strong, you will get nothing from me do you hear!"

"Saoirse, Leo. Come." Alessandro ordered them to face their interrogation.

Leo took Saoirse by the hand and squeezed it, which was not unnoticed by those watching. She looked up at where she assumed Leo's face was and smiled a nervous smile. Then just as it had before a flash of sight, she saw his face, his present face with the dirt and the stress and the fake confidence. He knew nothing of what had happened in that brief moment but he thought he saw her eyes shine brighter for a moment, just as they did when he visits her dreams.

"Step with both feet in the water and answer the questions truthfully," the voice was ice cold. She was led into the river and Leo was told to go a separate way. He was not happy and tried to argue but Saoirse told him to go on. She would be fine and would join him shortly.

"Saoirse Slamina. It is a pleasure to meet you in the flesh," she felt the hairs on her arms stand up. She didn't trust him, but then perhaps it was just fear. She had to be strong and brave!

"Tell me, would you do anything that was in your power to save Gandros and end the war and bring it back to prosperity?"

"If it was in my power I would do it."

"Swear it."

"I swear to do whatever I can."

"Excellent. Now step into the next river until you feel the ground beneath you give way. Then all you need to do is swim towards the warm water until you reach the entrance to our land and you will be able to stand."

"I can't swim. I never learnt!"

"Then you had better learn fast." He lifted her and threw her into the next section of river, where the ground gave way and she was completely submerged. She panicked and swam around in circles; she could feel the warm water and the cold. She wanted to follow the warm path but didn't know what to do; the current was dragging her further away. She needed air. Her lungs were burning. She really needed air. Her head was bursting with the pressure. She tried to stop herself but she opened her mouth and the water gushed in. Her movements slowed and she drifted further from the warmth.

Her mind flew gracefully to the family that had adopted her. She saw them standing over her in a hospital bed. They were crying. They looked so vulnerable, so weak, so defeated. Her mother fell onto her father's lap and hugged him. Her tears soaking his shoulder while his tears rolled carelessly down his face. She glided over to them and put her arms around them. They didn't know she was there, they couldn't see her but little did she know they felt calming warmth. Behind them were her Psychiatrist and another doctor.

"She hasn't been breathing on her own for a while now. She is brain dead, I am so sorry but there is nothing we can do. Have you made your decision?"

"Yes. We are ready. We have said good bye. You can turn off the machines. Our daughter deserves to be free." Her mother climbed onto the bed with her other body and her father held her hand. The doctor turned off the sound of the machines and quietly said he would be back shortly to talk about organ donation. They just nodded.

Saoirse didn't know what to think. Was she dead? Was she dying? Was this real? Was Gandros real? In a moment of blind panic she flew down and tried to shake her body awake. She screamed at her parents.

"I'm here. I'm here! I'm not ready to die! Please help me! I'm so scared! Help me!"

A strong arm pulled Saoirse away from her parents and her lifeless body. She could hear Leo screaming.

"Don't you dare let her die! If she dies I will kill you all! Saoirse! Sarah! Come back! We have come too far! Your story is not over yet! Is she breathing yet? What have you done to her? Don't you dare die on me!"

His voice was growing fainter and everything was going dark. What was the point in fighting anymore?

She couldn't see the faces of the Hoggronn Xzenny and even Alessandro as they tried to shield their smiles from onlookers. Her mind joined the darkness of her sight. She gave up.

To be continued…